Workhouse Prophecy

A Nottinghamshire Ghost Story

Workhouse Prophecy

A Nottinghamshire Ghost Story

PAM LITTLEWOOD

Beesthorpe Books

First published in Great Britain in 2001 by
Beesthorpe Books, Beesthorpe Hall Farm, Caunton,
Newark, Nottingham NG23 6AT

British Library Cataloguing-in-Publication Data
A catalogue record for this book is available from the
British Library

ISBN 0-9541750-0-X

Typeset and printed by Q3 Print Project Management Ltd,
Loughborough, Leics.

DEDICATION

This book is dedicated to my daughter Rachel and my son Matt.

ACKNOWLEDGEMENTS

I acknowledge the use of material from the Poll Book for 1826 for Newark.

Thanks to:

- Hilary Heason
- Jean Matthews
- Jean Maluta
- Peter Littlewood

CHAPTER ONE
Wilhelmina

1875

COLD fear crept up over Wilhelmina as she lay in her bed. She felt she had been woken by a sound but now, as she lay rigid between the sheets, apart from the thumping of her heart, there was silence. The full moon, aligning directly with the attic window, flooded the tiny room with light and illuminated the enamelled jug on the shelf like a beacon. The air was as chilled as the ice-house and Wilhelmina shivered. Erratic bursts of her breath hung in wispy clouds before her face.

Was someone in the room? Her eyes wide with fear, Wilhelmina forced herself to take in the familiar shapes. There was little to survey. On the iron bedstead her black work skirt and white apron lay neatly folded. From a peg behind the door hung her Sunday skirt, coat and hat and on the windowsill sat a stub of candle on a saucer. There was nothing out of place and no intruder. Perhaps it was just a rat she'd heard or could it be cockroaches? The fear held on to her – irrational and inexplicable.

Wilhelmina struggled to regulate her breathing but her heart seemed to be pumping too much blood through her veins and her ears thumped loudly. Her scalp tingled and the hairs on her arms stood out. Suddenly a groan emanated from the wall beside her; an agonized, bone chilling groan, and she drew her knees up and hugged herself, her teeth chattering and her body trembling. Could it be in the next room? As far as she knew it was empty and she'd never seen anyone go in there. As she stared across at the wall, dark stains began to appear. They gradually spread down and formed an irregular shaped stain on the floor, clearly visible in the eerie light. Slowly the wall began to bulge. The jug on the shelf flew across the room, shattering on the hard floor. The wall came nearer and nearer, filling the tiny attic bedroom. In disbelief, Wilhelmina's jaw dropped and her face contorted in terror. She filled her lungs with air and screamed. The scream filled her head and her whole being. It consumed her and became her but suddenly she was aware that the sound was not actually emanating from her. She was reduced to pathetic squeaks and sobs but still, from somewhere, the primeval scream continued.

To escape from the room was her only thought. She leapt from the bed but as her hand reached out for the door, the wall seemed to heave and burst in on her, spattering the sticky dark stains over her hair and night shift. The repulsive groans became louder, and the scream went on and on. As she tried to turn, her feet slipped in the dark liquid collected on the floor and she lurched back on the bed.

Blood! Blood was everywhere! A revolting, putrid smell invaded her nose and throat, causing her to gag. Fervently, she began to pray, fragmented snatches of prayer mingling with her sobs and pleas for help. 'Please God, please help me. Our Father which art in heaven – oh dear God, please help me'.

Suddenly the room subsided into silence but the relief was countered by the moon disappearing behind a heavy cloud and plunging Wilhelmina into a depth of palpable, evil darkness. Her chest tight with terror, she curled up in her bed and lay in a trembling state of shock, whimpering and whispering to God throughout the long, endless night.

When, at last, the first light spread across the sky and Wilhelmina dared to open her eyes, she raised herself and summoned all her courage. Gingerly, she put a foot to the floor. Nothing happened. The blood seemed to have gone but she was not going to be lulled into false hope. She knew she had not imagined the horrors of the night. Hardly daring to breathe, she tip-toed to the door and in one movement, opened it and shot through. She pinned herself against the far wall of the narrow corridor. There was the locked door to the next room, innocently facing her with none of its secrets on display; not a blister of paint nor a crack in the woodwork. Inching past, Wilhelmina never took her eyes off it. The next she knew she was hurling herself down the winding stairs and then tumbling down the back stairs until, on reaching the scullery door, her legs finally buckled and she crumpled to the floor.

Wilhelmina Waggonreider was not a woman given to the vapours. Known as Winnie to her friends, she was solid, somewhat coarse featured with brawny arms and big feet. Only recently she had floored a would-be romancer at the local fair. Emboldened by an unaccustomed tipple, he had tottered towards her and reached out to snatch a kiss, only to find himself on his back, staring at the sky and wondering just exactly what had happened. Wilhelmina was bold and sensible and had been the laundry maid at Beesthorpe Hall for three weeks, tirelessly filling and emptying the huge copper and turning the handle of the mangle in the wash-house. She was a hard-working, practical, no-nonsense girl.

Cook came bustling into the kitchen, tying her apron and tucking the last few whisps of grey hair into her cap. With breakfast on her mind, she reached for the range and caught sight of the last thing she would ever have expected to see – Winnie, a crumpled, quivering wreck on the floor in her night shift.

'What on earth? My dear girl whatever?' She didn't bother to finish, it being obvious that the girl was incapable of giving an answer.

3

Richard's heavy boots gave a satisfying clomping sound as he turned into the drive leading to Beesthorpe Hall. He had trudged through the village of Caunton in a sleepy daze and now, on the last leg of his daily walk to work, he was slowly waking up. The sound of his boots pleased him, as the cobbler had re-soled and heeled them only last evening. Richard had sat, bare-foot, in the dusty little shop, waiting whilst the task was completed before he could continue his walk home to the run-down farm near Norwell where his family lived.

Richard ranked somewhere in the middle of a boisterous family of eight. Home life was chaotic and a struggle. His elder brothers already worked on the small farm his father rented on Lord Middleton's estate so there was no place left for him there. When he was given the job as under-gardener at Beesthorpe Hall, Richard rejoiced in his good fortune. He always saw the positive side of life, was cheerful and stoical. His appearance was nothing special except for one thing. He had a tangle of wiry, red hair and the promise, in the course of time, of equally fiery side whiskers. As though attempting to calm down the tousled mass, Richard always wore a brown cap which clung on tenaciously in all weathers. He loved his family, his job and the countryside and was grateful for the meagre wages doled out to him each week by his employer, Captain Pollard.

Since Captain Pollard's arrival at Beesthorpe Hall, the head gardener had been sacked so Richard was now the only gardener. Yet no extra wages came his way – only extra responsibilities. His poor mother was always nagging him to ask for more money and he had, in a roundabout sort of way, but Captain Pollard had not responded.

Whisps of morning mist still clung to the beckside meadow as Richard picked up his stride on the driveway winding through the wooded parkland. The first sunrays burst through and lit up the flowering candles on the horse chestnuts. The flock of ewes began to stir themselves and embark on their morning search for new grass-shoots, and eager lambs rushed to fill their stomachs with warm milk.

Beesthorpe Hall came fully into view. The early light bathed the elegant windows and chimneys with a warmth and solid permanence. As Richard passed the lake a flash of blue caught his attention and he smiled as he watched the kingfisher embarking on an early breakfast. He started to whistle softly. It seemed a shame to wake the morning but the tune lifted his spirits and he was in no doubt that it was going to be a beautiful day.

By the time Richard had entered the iron gates and skirted around to the back kitchen door he was whistling merrily, as usual. 'Mornin' Cook. You got enough dry sticks for that range?' He stopped abruptly and stared, open mouthed at the sight of the crumpled Wilhelmina. Cook appeared in the scullery doorway with a blanket in her arms.

'Help me get her up, Richard – and don't you go looking at things you shouldn't.' she said sternly. 'Let me just cover her decent.' She draped the blanket around the girl and looked up impatiently for help from Richard. Together, they heaved Wilhelmina on to the nearest chair, where she lolled awkwardly against the table, still in shock.

'Is she ill?' Richard asked, hoping for a simple explanation. Cook made no answer as she patted, stroked and comforted the girl she barely recognised as the dependable laundry maid. Silently, Richard set about lighting the range and preparing some tea. After a while he mustered the courage to say what was on his mind.

'Do you think it's the same as the others?' he whispered to Cook.

She tightened her lips. 'It could be, but we'll hear what Winnie has to say first.'

Eventually, with much prompting as well as hot, sweet tea, the whole story did come out and Cook and Richard exchanged a serious look. The telling of the story in her own time and in the comfort of the now sun-filled, familiar kitchen gave Wilhelmina strength and as she came to the end she left no illusions as to the outcome of her ordeal. She would not stay one more night in the house. She was leaving.

'Now don't be hasty, Winnie' Cook pleaded. Captain Pollard promised that if this happened one more time, he would do something about it.'

'If this happened one more time? You mean it's happened before? And you didn't tell me?' Wilhelmina's tone was incredulous. She looked accusingly at Richard who held her gaze for only a moment before turning his head away.

'Well, the stories have never been as bad as this' Cook countered defensively 'and the other girls we always thought were a bit silly and, well – fanciful. But mostly we needed a good worker to stay. Too many have left, especially since Captain Pollard took the tenancy here.' The explanation trailed off.

The angular frame of Captain Pollard, dressed with his customary attention to detail, descended the main stairs to make his way to breakfast. He had yet to encounter his wife, although he had heard movements in her bedroom. If Cook got on with things he could be finished and have made his escape before she even came down. The prospect appealed to him. He hesitated on the bottom step, absently stroked his dark beard and checked the time with his pocket watch. He missed his old naval life. The ships and the sea and even the rough company was a life he had much preferred to this rural incarceration. He'd

6

had no idea that life actually living with his wife could be so miserable. Taking the tenancy of Beesthorpe Hall had been a bad decision. Mrs. Pollard made no secret of her detestation of the place and there seemed to be no end to the domestic crises of one kind or another.

Captain Pollard strode down the hall to the dining room, his precise steps echoing on the flagstones. He opened the door, fully expecting the aroma of freshly cooked bacon and hot coffee and his eyes went immediately to the table. It was not laid. With a sigh of exasperation he turned but coming into the room immediately behind him was Cook. Narrowly avoiding a collision, she wasted no time and hastily embarked on the tale.

'So, Captain Pollard, Sir,' Cook concluded. 'If you would be so kind, perhaps you could come through into the kitchen and speak to Wilhelmina. See for yourself, as it were.'

'Er. Well. Yes, I suppose I could do that. Yes. Lead on Cook.' Cook scurried off down the passage and Captain Pollard followed reluctantly behind. He sighed in exasperation. He was never at ease in the servants' quarters but this latest drama did indeed sound as though it could have repercussions.

In the kitchen, he listened to Wilhelmina's story again. Cook stood at her side with her arms folded, presenting a united front. Richard riddled and raked the range, outwardly silent but his mind working hard to put together half forgotten rumours and old tales. The Captain regarded Wilhelmina gravely. He could not fail to appreciate her distress and agreed that she was not the hysterical type. He patted her awkwardly on the shoulder, nodded as if making a silent decision and retreated to the dining room to await his breakfast.

Captain Pollard sat at the head of the table, silently awaiting the tirade which would come from his wife

7

when the events of the night were relayed to her. It was with glum resignation that he now viewed the day. Whatever he said, did or suggested would be wrong. Ultimately, it would, of course, be his fault because he had taken the tenancy of this beastly place which had yet to bring either of them any solace, comfort or happiness.

The door opened and Mrs. Pollard made her dignified entrance.

'Good morning, Edward.' She inclined her head graciously to her husband before her eyes rested on the unlaid table and her expression froze.

'Good morning, my dear – now don't distress yourself but we have had an incident and everything is in hand. Cook is preparing breakfast at this very moment and I am sure we will not be kept waiting long.'

Mrs. Pollard stood erect in the centre of the room, her hair pulled back as severely and as hard as her expression. She was determined not to relax or soften her stern features until a satisfactory explanation had been received. Her poor husband knew this, of course, the very same scenario having been played out many times before. He took a deep breath and embarked upon the story. Mrs. Pollard listened in stony silence except when particularly moved to exclaim 'Fiddlesticks!' or 'Poppycock!' Eventually, with a defiant swish of her skirts, she crossed the room to take her seat at the other end of the long table, from where she continued to regard her husband with contempt.

The expanse of empty table that lay between husband and wife was accurately indicative of their mutual regard. Never a passionate couple, their marriage had been as well suited to the enforced separations due to seafaring duties, as it was ill suited to the mundane domesticity now strangling the life out of their relationship.

Captain Pollard drummed his fingers on the table and ignored his wife's glare by gazing out of the window. The view was green and tranquil but failed entirely to instil in him any sense of purpose or belonging. He would willingly have exchanged it for the most tempestuous of seas. How he hated the country.

Mrs. Pollard made an effort to calm her feelings. Extreme agitation and annoyance only served to fuel her palpitations. She smoothed the folds of her morning dress and restricted herself to feelings of resentment that life was treating her so cruelly. She had lost count of how many times the dress had been mended. Her fingers played with a loose thread. Their retreat into the country, leaving the excitement of Bristol, had not been made with quite sufficient funds and consequently their acceptance into the county class had not materialised. She shuddered inwardly as she brought to mind the local farmers and their boring wives. They were way beneath her status, however they may go out of their way to be agreeable. She was, after all, the daughter of an Admiral, but somehow her husband, who had shown such promise for a glittering naval career, had never reached the heights to which she aspired. Her life here was intolerably lonely. And the house. How in the world could they have agreed to take the rental of such a cold, sombre place? There had been a problem with damp, mice and servants since the very first day. Nothing but problems. And now this. Ghosts. Of all things!

Cook eventually appeared carrying a heavily laden tray. 'Morning Ma'am. Sorry for the delay.' she mumbled, head down and hands hurriedly dealing utensils in all directions. Her unusually flushed cheeks and slightly breathless voice, not to mention her smoky aroma, indicated she had made all possible haste, but Mrs. Pollard did not notice. The breakfast was taken in crisp silence.

When Cook came to clear away, she decided to be bold and enquire directly. 'Have you made a decision yet Captain Pollard? What is to be done?'

'Yes Cook. Yes, I have decided. I shall write to the agent today. We must open up that room and, what is more, we shall ask for the help of the clergy in the matter.'

Mrs. Pollard, sitting perfectly still at her end of the dining table, rolled her eyes and spat out 'Ridiculous! What stuff and nonsense!'

Embarrassed, Captain Pollard turned to Cook and enquired 'What of Wilhelmina? How is she now?'

'Well, Sir, in a little while, when she has her strength back, she'll be walking down to Caunton to spend a few days with her friend, the seamstress. Probably for the best.'

'Ah. Now. I wonder if that would be wise. Gossip and tittle-tattle?' He raised his eyebrows as though his meaning was perfectly clear. 'You know how these things are so easily exaggerated.'

'I don't think, Sir, that it would be possible to stop her. Wilhelmina is a strong willed girl when she's made her mind up about something.' Cook drew a noisy intake of breath and shook her head.

'Very well, very well.' Captain Pollard left his chair and in two strides was looming over his long suffering servant. 'But now Cook, be sure to impress upon her the need for discretion. We don't want village gossip. And tell her the matter will be put right. And, er, if she feels able to resume her duties in a day or so, I will, er, of course, increase her wages'

A vicious sniff came from the other end of the table but Captain Pollard was careful to not look in that direction and, therefore, avoided his wife's disapproving face.

'Yes, Sir. Thank you, Sir'

Cook gathered the breakfast remains and stomped noisily down the flagstone passage with the tray piled high and the crockery balanced precariously. 'It's a wonder the words didn't stick in his throat' she grumbled. 'Never been known to increase anybody's wages. And if he did, she'd find a way of taking it back again! Penny to a pound he forgets he ever said that. Mean old skinflint.'

CHAPTER TWO
Jed

RICHARD picked up the hoe, balanced it on his shoulder and made his way to the walled garden. He chopped and hacked half-heartedly at a few weeds, his mind in turmoil from the events of the morning. The trouble was, nobody knew the proper story. He had dim recollections of his grandfather talking of the old days and hinting that something wicked had happened at Beesthorpe Hall but the rest was all hearsay, whispers and denials. And now Winnie, of all people.

He decided it was time he had a good chat with Jed. The old gamekeeper was old enough to remember and might tell the story if he had a mind to. Richard propped the hoe against the wall and made his way through the spinney towards Jed's house. Hovel would be a more accurate word for it and Richard was amused as he recalled Jed's spirited defence of his home in the face of opposition from Captain Pollard. It was a mud construction, with a crude door and window and thatched roof. Inside was just one room where he slept, cooked and ate but mostly Jed was outside anyway, wandering in the woods.

Jed had lived here for over fifty years. In his youth, he was known in the locality as the best poacher in Nottinghamshire. The Beesthorpe estate was owned by Samuel Bristowe, a young man then, and he had come to live at the Hall after inheriting from his uncle. He knew he had a problem with poachers, both at the lake and in the woods. He also knew that Jed was the main culprit. When Jed was offered the job of gamekeeper on the Beesthorpe estate, Samuel Bristowe had shown a shrewd perception which had paid dividends over the years. In exchange for his hut in the woods, regular wages and respect for his abilities, Jed had pursued poachers with the zeal of the converted. He had patrolled the Beesthorpe estate night and day, and with the aid of his old blunderbuss, had sent many a boy dancing home to Caunton with his backside full of shot.

Richard reached the hovel. It was a scene of decay, death and carnage. Being so old now, crippled and twisted with rheumatism, Jed no longer caught poachers, but vermin were an easier prey. The ground was littered with traps, nooses, hooks and bulging sacks. A bundle of rats tails was strung up alongside a couple of fox brushes and on a line between the trees hung a dozen or more dead crows, their feathers fluttering grimly in the breeze. A pile of half cured rabbit and mole skins lay tossed by the door. Richard wrinkled his nose. No wonder old Pollard wanted Jed and all this lot removed. But Jed had reminded Captain Pollard that he was not the owner, merely a tenant like himself, and he had been granted permission to live there for the rest of his days by young Mr. Bristowe 'a gentleman, just as his father before him, God rest his soul.'

Richard called out 'Jed! You there, Jed?' He banged on the door and then opened it and stooped to enter. Against the far wall, the crude, makeshift bed was covered with a magnificent blanket of rabbit skins. Of all the disgusting things that Jed lived with, this alone, was a thing of beauty and Richard coveted it. He reached out and stroked the soft fur which had been painstakingly cured and stitched to make a counterpane for a king. The fire was cold and the recess empty of sticks. That meant Jed was out somewhere in the woods – sticking.

Richard emerged, blinking in the light, and made his way further up the spinney. Bright May sunshine pene-trated the canopy of newly opened leaves and as he strode, he crushed carelessly the first of the bluebells. He heard the snapping of the sticks and turned towards the sound. Jed's bent, misshapen form was at odds with the leafy glade, bursting as it was with young fresh foliage, and although he heard Richard's approach, he continued with his task of retrieving and snapping dead wood to take home for kindling.

The young gardener stood quietly on the edge of the clearing. For a moment he watched the old man in the familiar, black hat with the grey hair straggling beneath, and the ragged coat of many years service, tied around with string. He understood Jed's need to carry on living his life in the way he always had. The world might be changing but Jed would be answerable to no-one. Except that as he aged, life became ever more difficult. The farmers' wives brought him broth and bread and Cook often sent Richard out with leftovers from the Pollard dining table – without Mrs. Pollard's knowledge, of course. Now that the weather was improving, life should be a little easier for him. 'At least he's made it through the winter' Richard thought 'He'll be alright til the next one.'

'Mornin' Jed.'

'What you be wantin' this time o'day? Don't weeds grow in May no more?' Jed's gruff voice and manner was always to the point. He stuffed twigs in the sack and, still bent nearly double, lurched forward, dragging his leg and the sack of sticks. His chest crackled and wheezed and he coughed up and spat out.

'You got enough goose grease for your chest?'

'Yep'

Moving nearer, and catching the rank odour emanating from him, Richard had no cause to doubt Jed's word. 'Let me carry that for you. Here, I have it.'

'Don't need no help.' Jed peered up at Richard, his watery old eyes still intense and missing nothing. 'What's up?'

'It's Winnie, you know, the new laundry maid. She's had a terrible fright. Saw horrible things and heard screams. Up in the attic. She won't stay now.' Richard sighed heavily. 'Something happened didn't it, Jed – a long time ago – something bad? Was it in that locked room?'

With his back still bowed, Jed lifted his head like an old tortoise to look at the sky. Oblivious to the dewdrop on the end of his nose which finally dropped off, he simply said 'Aye'.

'Will you tell me the story then? I think it's time we knew.'

'No good come of it then, and no good'll come of it now.' Jed took hold of the sack and started dragging it home. Richard followed, collecting bundles of sticks as he went. He knew not to push Jed.

They settled the sticks in the recess and got the fire going. Jed put the water on to boil and suddenly said, 'T'were Kitty Wilkinson that spoiled it all. It were a well run house – Mr. Bristowe such a gentleman and his wife so young and delicate. He were well thought of hereabouts but afterwards – well it affected us all see.'

Jed eased himself into his chair by the fireside and watched the flames flickering. 'Guilt is a terrible thing. Your grandfather and I – we only did what we thought was right.'

'My grandfather? Billy White from Caunton?

Jed nodded. 'Only we knew what happened. Why the ghost is walking.'Richard settled himself on the floor, hugging his knees. The silence was broken only by the crackling sticks and Jed's wheezy breath. Richard leaned back against the wall and patiently waited. The old man would take his time, as he always did.

After a while Jed continued. 'We all felt it. Mrs. Bristowe became ill with the strain an' all, and Mr. Bristowe, he got us all together in the stable courtyard one day. Said he knew the whole county were talkin', but it were affecting his wife bad, so from that moment on we

15

were forbidden to speak about it. If we did, we'd be sacked. Simple as that.' The gnarled hands, painfully contorted, came together in his lap and entwined themselves anxiously as the memories of those distant times became clearer. 'Old Bristowe was a good man, but you knew he meant what he said. You just knew.'

'Surely people didn't just forget about it, did they?' Richard asked.

'No, they didn't. But you have to remember boy, times was hard, bread was dear and we would have starved 'cept for the squire letting us take the rabbits. And lucky we was to get 'em. We needed our jobs bad – so, we just didn't talk about it. Didn't dare. After a time we just kind o' didn't think about it. Best left forgotten. Now o' course, there's only about me alive to remember.'

The long speech brought on the rattling chest and after a paroxysm of coughing and a few sips of hot tea, Jed gazed wistfully into the fire. 'You see, I didn't do as I should have – and now there's a price to pay. But I do remember. I remember she were the prettiest thing I ever did see. The face of an angel. But God made her pay cruelly for her mistakes.'

'Was that Kitty? Tell me about Kitty, Jed.'

'Ah Kitty. I'll tell you the story but the Lord knows it's not a pretty one.' The weather-beaten old face grew wistful as he gazed into the fire and searched his memory of fifty years ago. 'T'would have been better if Kitty Wilkinson had never set foot at Beesthorpe Hall.' Jed's voice was barely a whisper. 'Never set foot.'

CHAPTER THREE
Inheritance

1824

IT was over fifty years earlier, in the month of May, that the old man lay in the four-poster bed, propped up on numerous pillows. Weak sunshine filtered through the half closed window drapes. Thomas Bristowe, squire and gentleman, Justice of the Peace and landowner, reluctant to relinquish his hold on life and hand over command of his estate, nevertheless lay dying. The housekeeper fussed by the bedside. For days she had steadily trudged back and forth, up and down the stairs, bringing things into the room and taking them out again. She had created a trail of uneaten food, bowls of water, towels and chamber pots. The doctor called daily but lately only to check the patient's pulse, note the deterioration of his breathing and report to the family. Slow death could be very tedious.

At the age of eighty three, Thomas Bristowe's life on earth was almost over and the hereafter awaited him. He had never enjoyed the pleasures or responsibilities of a wife but with four nephews and three nieces, all hopeful of a stake in the inheritance, the house was full of relatives awaiting his demise. Carriages came and went and candle-lit vigils were held by the bedside. No-one knew the content of the will but the ultimate prize of the Beesthorpe estate had drawn them all to uncle Thomas for years. He had, of course, been well aware of this and had enjoyed himself in his latter years, stringing them all along with veiled hints here and there, as the fancy took him. Now they congregated in the drawing room making polite, subdued conversation. Each in a state of half excitement that they may be the fortunate one, and half dread that they may not, they awaited the inevitable.

John McCready, an under-butler and the old man's personal valet, quietly ascended the stairs and entered the bedroom. The doctor looked up as he gently replaced the limp hand of the sick man on the counterpane. He picked up his bag and left the room. McCready stood by the bedside. Suddenly, Thomas Bristowe opened his eyes and looked directly at his valet. With great effort, he turned his head to the bedside table and rested his gaze on the full bottle of laudenum. Back and forth his eyes went. No words came but the meaning was clear.

John McCready could not help his unnerving appearance. His unusual height and stick-thin frame was topped by a pock-scarred face and his mistrustful countenance and reluctance to speak gave him an air of insolence. He wore an invisible armour – an impenetrable shield developed over the years and he cared for no-one except Thomas Bristowe. This influential man had given him a chance when all others had mocked and ridiculed him. McCready would always be grateful and he hated to see this all powerful man reduced to the frailty of old age, impotent in the face of death. His hand reached out for the bottle.

The old man's breath came in painful gasps. As McCready put his hand behind his head to lift him, he opened his eyes and the two men locked in a gaze of understanding. As the nephews arrived to group around the bed, he discreetly retrieved the bottle and retreated to the back of the room. Faintly, the distant sound of the passing bell, ringing at Caunton church, carried down the valley.

Tenants and villagers, as well as local society, turned out to give Thomas Bristowe a respectful funeral. The vicar

18

spoke at length of his humanity and the fair manner in which he had discharged the responsibility of his duties as Lord of the Manor. The coffin was laid in the family vault in the Church of St. Andrew in Caunton.

One by one the family carriages rattled back down the driveway to Beesthorpe Hall. The hopeful inheritors gathered in the vast new dining room, built by uncle Thomas only a few years earlier. The Georgian windows extended almost from floor to ceiling, and from his position over the mantelpiece, Uncle Thomas' portrait commanded the view down to his beloved Lockabeck meadow.

The atmosphere was tense. The normally garrulous family fell silent, uncomfortable in each others company and unwilling to look directly upon one another. The family lawyer entered the room and laid his papers out on the table. Over his tight collar, his reedy voice struggled for volume in the echoing, high-ceilinged room but the profound silence into which he spoke rendered him audible.

After the preamble of the will, he finally came to the crucial part. 'and I, therefore, leave my house, estate and lands at Beesthorpe, in their entirety, to my nephew, Samuel Bristowe, on the understanding that he keeps all tenants and staff as are at present employed, for a minimum of five years.' The lawyer stopped to draw breath and looked up from the document. He was met with a wall of disbelieving faces staring back at him – motionless, speechless and uncomprehending.

Samuel Bristowe sat perfectly still and slowly exhaled. He was stunned. His cousins turned to stare at him, some accusingly, some hurt and some plainly distressed. The lawyer continued to the end and then stood to leave. 'Which one of you is Samuel Bristowe?'

Samuel raised his hand.

'I shall present myself here in the morning at eleven of the hour to discuss matters further with you. Good-day, ladies and gentlemen.'

A few murmured 'Congratulations, Samuel' and 'No money worries for you now,' chokingly articulated the family shock. The whole estate and fortune to Samuel – no-good, forget tomorrow, impetuous, twenty three year old Samuel.

The meeting with the lawyer the next day was a simple matter. The retention of existing staff was easy enough except in the case of the butler, who was to be retired with a small sum and John McCready to be promoted accordingly. Samuel was puzzled by this as, frankly, he found this particular man slightly distasteful and posessing a rather odd manner. Yet his uncle had liked him so, that being good enough for Samuel, and the will being most explicit, McCready was duly informed of his new post. The young employer shook his hand warmly and received in return a rare smile. It was a good basis on which to start the relationship of squire and butler.

Samuel was eager to study the map of the estate as marked out by the lawyer. There was a solid block of acreage at Beesthorpe and then other parcels of land in surrounding parishes. He strode out to the stables – his stables. A lad was carrying water across the yard. 'Can you saddle me a horse?' Samuel asked.

'I can, Sir. Which one is it to be?'

They entered the arched doorway of the stable block. Inside, everything was in scrupulous order with the horses standing in clean stalls amongst the pervading sweetness of good hay.

'Who is in charge here?'

'I am the coachman, Sir. Jeremiah Jennings.'

Samuel looked again at the boy. 'How old are you?'

'Eighteen, Sir.' Jeremiah smiled. 'Mr. Bristowe was well satisfied with my abilities.'

Samuel felt dubious. 'Well now, which horse do you recommend to ride out?'

'Well, we've the cob for the trap and a steady ride. And then we've the two blacks for the carriage and a fiery pace. They're pretty headstrong, though I must warn you.'

'I think, Jeremiah, that for the occasion of my first ride out on my own land, it must be done in spirited style.' Samuel was just beginning to allow himself a tinge of excitement and self importance.

'In that case, Sir, I'll saddle Henry. Rupert can be the very devil if taken away from his pair.'

White clouds chased across a blue sky as Samuel galloped off on his new mount, through Caunton and out on the Norwell road. Labourers in the fields looked up and rested on their hoes as they watched from beneath their wide-brimmed hats. The thoroughbred, straining for his head, pounded down the road and Samuel was exhilerated with the exertion of controlling him. At the Bathley ford bridge he managed to rein back and take out the map from his pocket. With difficulty, he studied it to make out where his land lay. The first farmstead he came to was small and muddy. Half grown children drove old sows across the squelching yard into the pigstye and protesting geese honked indignantly as they scattered from his path. The horse stamped and Samuel dared not attempt to dismount. He introduced himself as the new landlord to the surprised farmer, raised his crop in salute to his wife in the doorway and careered off down the road to Willoughby. From there he cut back to Kersall and the turnpike road to the coaching inn at Caunton Common farm.

By now, the horse had almost run himself out and Samuel was able to halt on the old Beesthorpe common.

After the Enclosures Act, and much haggling and dispute between local landowners, ownership of the common land had finally gone to his uncle. Now it was Samuel's, as was almost all the land he could see from this good vantage point.

'Henry, my friend, that was quite a gallop.' Samuel was breathing hard as he spoke to the horse and slapped his sweated neck. Henry's mud spattered sides heaved and he was blowing hard as Samuel finally relaxed in the saddle. A wide smile gave way to a full throated laugh as his enviable situation and extrordinary good fortune hit home. Up to this moment, Samuel's future had been uncertain. He had trained as a lawyer, completing his studies belatedly and only due to the indulgence of his uncle who had met the mounting debts incurred whilst at Cambridge. Eventually, the spate of gambling and drunkenness had run its course and the necessity of earning a living had loomed nearer. Now that could be put off forever. His living and future were assured. His thoughts turned to Sarah, his cousin and life-long friend. A house like Beesthorpe Hall needed a mistress.

Samuel touched Henry lightly with his heel and they walked along the cart track. Flocks of sheep dotted the rolling hillsides and cows, mostly brown and splashed with white, grazed amongst the buttercups in the beckside meadows. It was a magnificent view. Down in the valley, the houses of Maplebeck clustered around the pointed spire of the church and smoke curled up enticingly from the chimneys. On a distant hillside a well loaded waggon pulled by work horses, threaded down the track on the hedge side. To the right the hamlet of Kersall clung to the hillside. From this high point, Samuel could make out the sails of the mills at Maplebeck, Caunton and Kersall as they turned in lazy unison in the light breeze.

Picking up the driftway, the track took Samuel back to Beesthorpe along the centuries old route. He dismounted at the top of the spinney and led Henry through the tangle of low boughs. No birds were disturbed, no game got up. Samuel realised he had not seen a rabbit or a hare all afternoon and it struck him as odd. He skirted the home farmstead and, still leading Henry, came around to the stables. Jeremiah heard the sound of hooves on the flagstoned courtyard and came out. His face registered displeasure at the sight of the sweat-lathered horse and Samuel felt a twinge of guilt.

'You were right. He is headstrong. Glad I didn't take the other one.' Samuel handed over the reins and turned to go back to the house as Jeremiah scowled and led Henry into the stall where he began to rub him down vigorously with straw. Turning back, Samuel said 'I presume you are familiar with the journey to Twyford?' Jeremiah nodded.

'Then have the carriage ready and we shall leave at nine, tomorrow.

CHAPTER FOUR
Beesthorpe

SARAH felt herself tingling with excitement at the prospect of seeing her home for the first time. She leaned forward to catch the first glimpse as her new husband sat back in the seat, smug in the knowledge that she would love it and would, therefore, love him all the more for being the provider of such a prize.

Samuel and Sarah's lives had entered a whirlwind phase since his return to Twyford after the demise of his uncle and his unexpected inheritance. His sudden proposal had taken both the families by surprise as Sarah was the daughter of his mother's brother. In less than one month, Samuel had become a wealthy landowner and a proud husband. Their wedding, just the previous day, had been a happy occasion, and Samuel was delighted to see that the flush of excitement was still on his bride's cheeks as the carriage neared the gates and Sarah took her first look at Beesthorpe Hall.

'Oh, Samuel.' she breathed. 'It is so beautiful. So elegant.'

Samuel helped her down from the carriage and proudly watched as her eyes took in every detail. McCready opened the front door and emerged between the porch columns to welcome the master and mistress. Like an old friend, Samuel shook his hand and he stiffly bowed to Sarah before ushering her through the door. Mrs. Welby, the housekeeper, stood in the hallway and curtsied as they entered.

'Welcome to Beesthorpe Hall, Ma'am. I've laid the fire in the bedroom and the drawing room. These big old rooms need cheering up even at this time of year. I can bring the tea in as soon as you wish.'

Sarah found Mrs. Welby's mature practicality reassuring. She knew nothing of housekeeping and would need all her help. Of McCready she was less sure.

It was with great pride that Samuel embarked on a tour of the house for his bride. They rushed from room to room, laughing and planning as they went.

'This can be your sitting room and that can be the drawing room and of course this' he opened the mahogany double doors with a flourish, 'is the ballroom. Which would you prefer – a summer ball or a winter one? Or both, perhaps?' Samuel seized his wife and danced the length of the room with her. Their laughter echoed through the house. In the kitchen, Mrs. Welby looked up from her cooking and listened with delight to hear the happy sound. Even McCready smiled.

'Tell me about uncle Thomas.' Sarah said as she stood before the portrait in the dining room. The table was laid for the supper Mrs. Welby was preparing at that very moment. Intricate candelabra supporting tall candles shone in the centre of the table, whilst delicate china and silver cutlery graced the place settings.

'From what I understand, when Uncle Thomas bought this estate forty years ago, it was in a sorry state of disrepair – dereliction even. I think that could be said of the farms as well as the house. Ever since that time, he spent his entire energies on improvements, to make it a profitable estate. The house was extended – the ballroom and this dining room were added – and new windows and roof repairs throughout. Oh and of course the garden and park is in the grand style of Capability Brown, no less.'

'And he left it all to you, Samuel. Why do you think he did that?'

'I wish I could answer. I suppose he liked me but now that I consider it, I must have sorely tried his patience on many occasions.'

McCready announced that dinner was served and the young master and mistress took their places at each end of the long table. Self conscious but happy, they enjoyed the meal and at the end Samuel requested McCready to ask Mrs. Welby to step through.

'Thank you Mrs. Welby, for our most excellent first dinner together here.' Samuel said. 'I know that Mrs. Bristowe and I will be happy here at Beesthorpe.'

Middle aged and with a flurry of extra rolls and wrinkles, Mrs. Welby's face broke out in pleasure for the recognition of the work she had put in to make the house and the meal a success for her new mistress.

'I wonder if there is another way you could help us. As I am sure you will realise, we must find for Mrs. Bristowe a lady's maid. Before we search further afield, do you know of a local girl who could be suitable?'

Mrs. Welby considered for a moment before her face brightened. 'As it happens, Sir, I think I do. Jenny Cocking from Kersall is a good girl, quiet and decent, and just like her mother, a good needlewoman. She's been helping out the seamstress in Caunton lately. I don't know for sure – but I think she might be very suitable.'

Samuel turned to McCready. 'Can you arrange for her to come to see Mrs. Bristowe tomorrow?'

'I can, Sir.'

Sarah watched McCready and was at a loss to make up her mind. He had such a withdrawn, slightly sinister manner yet although he made himself perfectly agreeable to Samuel, not once had he looked directly at her. She had the uneasy feeling that the butler would not prove to be her best ally in the first period of her life at Beesthorpe.

Jenny Cocking proved to be an accomplished seamstress with a quiet manner. Both Sarah and Samuel took a liking to her and hoped that she would be suitable. After a week's trial, they knew their first impression had been correct and Sarah was relieved that she turned out to be both capable and dependable. An attic bedroom was allocated to her but as her home at Kersall was barely a half hour's walk away, it was agreed she could have a few hours off most Sundays to see her mother. Jenny, too was wary of McCready and felt uncomfortable in his presence, so she mostly conversed with Mrs. Welby and gradually the household settled into a well-run routine.

The young Bristowes were welcomed into both the local and county society. Samuel spent his time familiarising himself with his estate. That times were hard for farmers and labourers he had no doubt. The price of wheat had fallen from its peak during the wars with the French but it was propped up by the imposition of the Corn Laws. All well and good to protect the home market but not allowing for a labourer to work hard for every day of the week and still be unable to feed his family. As he rode through the villages, Samuel noticed the gaunt faces of the ragged children and it bothered him. It also bothered him when the parish constable called to inform him of the dues he must pay under the Poor Law Act.

'This money is distributed to families where the head of household is in work, yet not earning enough to eat?' Samuel had never addressed social issues at first hand before, at least none beyond his own gambling and debt. The constable nodded. He could have told him that the farmers were failing to pay decent wages, and that in turn they paid landowners such as Samuel high rents. He didn't though. He saved his breath.

Lord of the Manor of Beesthorpe. When he thought about it, Samuel puffed out his chest. Except that Beesthorpe consisted only of the main house, two brick farmhouses and a handful of mud cottages. There used to be a school here once, he was told, and a chapel, but no more. The nearby village of Caunton served for most needs and there the Lord of the Manor was James Hole, a businessman and maltster with a fine house and brewery in Newark.

Before long the Bristowes were invited by Mr. & Mrs. Hole to attend a formal dinner at the Manor. Sarah dressed in her new gown of yellow silk and Jenny styled her hair, sweeping it up and teasing out some soft ringlets. A white feather muff and stole completed the effect and Samuel stood in the hallway, transfixed as Sarah descended the stairs. Unable to hide her excitement and pleasure, she approached her husband and offered her cheek for a kiss of approval. 'I think,' said Samuel 'that I am a very fortunate man indeed.' Sarah fingered the brass buttons of his black evening coat and straightened the pristine white stock. 'I am truly eager for us to take our place in the county society, Samuel, but I have also to confess to feelings of trepidation in view of the high company we are keeping this evening.' Samuel stood rigidly in his formal coat and constricting stock but he smiled encouragingly as he took his young wife's arm to lead her out to the coach.

It was an important social gathering attended by good county families – the Burnells from Winkburn Hall, the Dennisons from Ossington and the Suttons from Kelham were among the guests. Sarah tried to hide her feelings of unease and concentrated on noticing how everything was done so that when her turn came to be a social hostess, she would not let her husband down on some trivial point of etiquette. Endless courses of rich food were relayed from the kitchen – soup, fish, game pies, venison and exotic fruits.

The ladies retired from the table, leaving the gentlemen to their cigars, port and politics. Samuel listened politely for a time before bringing up the subject of the high cost of the Poor Rate.

'Damned iniquitous!' Mr. Dennison retorted. 'Great sums of money paid out each week for nothing. No work in return. Nothing to show for it but families increasing in size all the time. Always more mouths to feed!'

'Encourages laziness, to my mind.' said Mr. Sutton.

'How can that be?' said Samuel. 'I know of labourers working all hours on farms for six days a week, to take home nine shillings. A loaf of bread costs over ten pence each, so how does he feed himself, a wife and seven children?'

Col. Burnell nodded and puffed on his cigar. 'It's the price of wheat that's caused it all, Samuel. I know you're new to all this but you must know that the price has fallen from 126 shillings to 45 shillings a quarter.'

'Yes, Sir, I am aware and shouldn't we, as landowners, be reducing rents and finding other ways of feeding the needy without encouraging dependency.'

'Rents have been reduced. By twenty per cent in some cases. We can't risk our estates for a few profligate farmers, Samuel. And we can't be held to account for their not paying enough to their workers to cover the high cost of bread. They pay the poor rates too, you know.' Col Burnell smiled benignly, as to a child.

Samuel pressed on. 'We should be doing more. We should work towards a change in the system.' Carried away as he was with his argument, he banged his fist on the table and failed to notice the chill silence of disapproval descending upon the table. At best it was condescension to an inexperienced squire – at worst it was open hostility. Trails of cigar smoke hung between them like a barrier.

'I think, young man' said Mr. Sutton icily, 'that you may be endeavouring to reduce the guilt of your inheritance by laying it at our door. We landowners can hardly be held to blame for your sudden wealth and social conscience.'

James Hole cleared his throat as he stubbed out his cigar. He picked up the bottle of port and re-filled Mr. Sutton's glass. 'Gentlemen, we must not rebuff the opinions of this young man. He has much to learn, I'm sure, but social distress of the lower classes is a scourge of our time and one which will require change of some kind. We must ensure that it is the right change.' He looked at Samuel and his mouth smiled but his eyes did not. 'Now, gentlemen. If you are ready, perhaps we should rejoin the ladies.'

Sarah chattered as the coach swayed along the roadway. 'Did you notice the fine furniture, Samuel – and the quality of the window drapes? They must surely have come from London.' Only when she had finished recounting an itinerary of the contents of the house did she notice that her husband's manner was inattentive and pensive. 'Are you listening, Samuel? Is anything wrong?'

As they lay in the four poster, Samuel finally found a way of putting into words how he felt. 'I've never really noticed the poor before. Of course, I know they're always there but I never questioned how their lives came to be so. Now I see them, on my land and in my houses. Children barefoot and coughing – pinched faces and a look of hunger about them. And who cares about their future?' Samuel lay silently and then turned and snuffed out the candle. In the dark he continued 'And now I've spoken out of turn with men of importance and influence. They won't listen to me in future.'

Sarah snuggled up sleepily. 'I'm sure they will one day. In time.'

Young Jed Smith lay flat in the mud, his face pressed down so that water oozed up and threatened to trickle down his nose and throat. He had laid there for an hour, waiting, hiding and hoping his luck would change. The feeling in his arm, extended out in front of him, was beginning to go. Numbness through immobility crept over him. The bright afternoon sunlight penetrated the water and played out a pattern on his hand beneath, tirelessly reflecting the minute ripples of the surface. It was mesmerising. If only it would have the same effect on a passing trout, he could do what he came to do and go home.

His eyes caught the dark shadow lazily approaching. The fish glided nearer, inquisitively exploring the immobile hand. Using only the slightest of movement, Jed began to tickle the underside of the speckled brown trout. Suddenly, his hand shot up and flipped the fish out of the water and into the reeds. Quickly hoisting himself out of the sucking mud, Jed picked up the waggling fish and retreated back to the dense lakeside cover. Knowing how pleased his mother would be, he smiled as he looked down at his prize, still gulping air and flicking its tail from side to side in vigorous death throes. He managed to stuff it into the bag tied to his waist and crawled back to the safety of the steep banks of the beck. The water felt good as he splashed the mud from his hands and face.

Jed didn't usually work out in the daylight. Mostly his poaching took place in the dark, setting snares and traps, but the rabbit numbers were low this summer and he had taken to raiding the fishponds. The best time for tickling was mid-afternoon and for weeks now he had been successful in the deep pools dotted along the beck. He knew almost every individual trout there, had even given them names such as Long Tail and Big Speckle, and one by one, he had caught them all. Now if he wanted fish he had to go to the lake beneath the big house and it was risky. He decided not to tell his mother where this one came from. They both knew, only too well, the penalty for poaching.

Jed retreated back to Caunton via the steep, densely covered banks of the beck. If he heard voices, he could

31

blend into the foliage and not move a muscle. Many times men passed within feet of him, oblivious of his presence. Jed left the safety of the stream and sneaked up the hedgerow past the mill. Beyond, on the outskirts of the village, was the derelict cottage that was his home. The tiny dwelling with the leaky roof and draughty windows was always full to bursting with children, all dark haired and dark eyed, like himself. His mother did her best but since his father had died some years ago, he and his brother Ben, had tried to supplement the poor rate payment which was doled out so grudgingly each week by the constable. Without their efforts, it would have been near starvation for them all. As it was, Ben and Jed became the best poachers in Nottinghamshire. But now with Ben gone, it was all up to Jed.

His mother looked up as she heard the click of the latch. Her clothes were little more than rags but most worn out was her face. Her hair, prematurely grey, was pulled loosely back from her careworn brow and her eyes reflected resigned sadness. Nevertheless, she registered pleasure at the sight of her second eldest son. When he pulled the fish from the bag her heart lurched in her chest and she bit her lip. Passing a hand over her forehead, she whispered 'Not the lake, Jed. Please don't tell me you went to the lake in broad daylight.'

'No, mother. The pools.' Jed lied. 'I told you there are hundreds of fish in the pools.'

The look of fear was deep in his mother's eyes and Jed went to her side and put a hand on her shoulder. 'Don't worry. Nothing will happen to me.' With all the optimism of youth he cheerfully picked up the fish and took it outside for gutting.

Jeremiah raked off the clean straw from the stable bedding and then forked the pungent manure into the wheelbarrow. 'Morning, Jeremiah.' Samuel called out.

'Morning, Sir.'

'Jeremiah, I have to ask you a question to which I think I know the answer.' Samuel leaned on the stall gate and Henry came up to nuzzle him. 'Since coming here, I have noticed that, unlike other estates upon which I have ridden, there is very little, if indeed any, evidence of game of either fur or feather. Do you know if poaching has always happened here, even in my uncle's time, or is it just recently?'

'I wouldn't know, Sir.' Jeremiah evaded. 'Perhaps you should ask in the village.'

For a while, Samuel watched his young coachman pitching the manure before he thoughtfully retreated back to the house. Jeremiah straightened up and watched him go.

That Sunday, after church service, Samuel and Sarah passed a few moments conversation with Mr. & Mrs. Hole. Samuel put the same question to James Hole.

'Hah! We've had the same problem in the past and the only way to stop it is to get yourself a good gamekeeper. Catch 'em at it. It'll be the Smith boy, I'll be bound. His brother has been transported already. Tried his hand on Lord Middleton's estate. That was a serious mistake. Lord Middleton's gamekeepers are keen as mustard. Found himself in Nottingham gaol and now he's bound for Australia.'

Some weeks later, Samuel stood at the library window and did what he did most days – he surveyed his land. He admired the lake and the park and tried to imagine the beauty of the trees with another twenty years growth on them. He felt sure it would be twenty happy years he would spend here at Beesthorpe. He didn't see anything specific to catch his attention but his eyes were drawn to the reeds by the lake. A movement of some kind. Perhaps it was a fox after the mallards. Having little better to do, he strolled down to see if anything was there.

Samuel trod carefully on the tussocks and parted the reeds silently as he skirted the perimeter of the lake. Just on the point of turning back, he spotted the feet. Worn out boots poked out from between clumps of bog grass. Approaching from behind, Samuel saw the boy lying flat, concentrating on the fish about to come into his hand. He was virtually standing over him by the time Jed saw his shadow looming up in the lake and spun around.

' What's your name, boy?'

Jed remained silent. Still on the ground, he saw that the squire was unarmed. He thought quickly. He would make a run for it. In one movement he was up and pushing past Samuel, only to pull up short as he found himself facing the prong of a pitchfork and the belligerent face of farmer Todd. 'No you don't, boy.'

Addressing Samuel, he said 'I was working in Little Croft, Sir. An' I thought I saw something by the lake myself. Then I see you come by. Lookin'. I reckoned it might be him.'

Jed was marched up to the stables and locked in the feed shed. The constable was sent for. 'What is to happen now?' Samuel asked him.

'First, he walks to Southwell to the House of Correction. From there he'll go to Nottingham where he'll be found guilty and, if he's lucky, transported.' Turning to Jed he grinned and said 'Like as not, you'll be breaking stones in Australia with your brother.'

Samuel watched as Jed's wrists were manacled together and a chain attached. The constable mounted his horse and yanked the chain. The boy stumbled forward and so in a series of painful jerks, Jed's fateful journey to Southwell began.

Back in the house, Samuel rang the bell for Mrs. Welby. When he had told her the story, he asked her directly. 'What of this family? Is there real hardship there or are they just rogues?'

'Hard to say really. The farmers have no time for the older boys and hardly ever give them work – because of the stealing they say. But a widow with so many mouths to feed – well, I wouldn't even like to try. She must have been grateful for any extra food, no matter where it came from.' Tutting and shaking her head, Mrs. Welby returned to the kitchen.

That evening Samuel discussed the day's events with Sarah. 'I feel badly about that poor woman having two of her sons deported. How will she manage?'

Sarah watched her husband pacing up and down and listened attentively. 'The poor don't have a choice, Samuel.' she said. 'People like you make the decisions that change their lives. If you have not made the right decision, my dear, then you do have the power to change it.'

'What do you mean? How can I change anything?'

'If you feel as strongly as you say, you can go to South-well and bring the boy home.' Samuel stared at his wife. 'You could drop the charges.' she explained.

'I would be very unpopular with the other landowners.'

'You didn't hesitate to speak your mind at the dinner party.'

'And regretted it.'

'So uncle Thomas left you all this so that you could fall into line with society and never consult your own social conscience?'

Samuel felt himself becoming indignant before realising that his wife was right. But she had not yet finished. 'Uncle Thomas cared about people, about those less fortunate. That is why he included in his will that the staff were to be retained. And he chose you to carry on

35

the estate after him. Perhaps he knew you better than you know yourself.'

Samuel was stunned. As he considered his wife's words his brow became furrowed with deep lines. The implications of what was being suggested could have far reaching consequences and he would be forced to face and defend them. Finally, the frown disappeared as he said 'You are right. I'll go to Southwell tomorrow.'

As instructed, Jeremiah kept the horses to a good pace, all the way to Southwell. As they pulled up the hill into the town, the huge stone archway over the door into the House of Correction imposed its formidable presence over the green. Samuel rapped on the studded door with his cane and the sound echoed deep within. He was taken to the warden, who listened to what he had to say and then shook his head.

'This is unheard of. Poaching is a very serious matter.'

'But if I say he wasn't poaching, if I refuse to testify against him in court, then you have no case. Take me to see the prisoner.'

A more dejected sight Samuel had never seen. The young man sat in a filthy cell. Dank and airless, with only a high grid through which weak sunlight filtered, it seemed to have sucked the life out of him. As Jed raised his head to see the squire standing in the doorway, his dark eyes locked with Samuel's in fiery resentment. Samuel indicated for the warden to leave.

'How old are you, Jed?'

Jed shrugged. 'Twenty two or thereabouts.'

Samuel was surprised. He looked so much younger. 'You knew when you came to the lake what would happen if you were caught. You knew because it happened to your brother. How could you do this to your mother?'

Jed's back stiffened as his resentment intensified. How could he know what their lives were like? Standing there with his fancy clothes and full belly.

'It is wrong to steal.' Samuel continued.

'Is it wrong to send bairns to bed, wailing with hunger?' Jed spat back. 'Taking a fish wasn't taking food off your plate, was it? But it kept my family from starving. Not that the likes of you ever think about that.' With nothing to lose, Jed's face showed all the bitterness he felt towards the young squire who occupied his place of priviledge with so little thought for others.

Samuel felt uncomfortable but he tried to sound harsh. 'You will not go to Nottingham for trial and you will not be deported. You will come home with me but I tell you straight, Jed Smith, if I so much as lose one more rabbit, I'll hold you responsible. Do you hear? Warden!' Samuel banged on the door. 'Give me those release papers to sign. We're leaving.'

Warily, Jed followed Samuel out through the prison door. 'Get up the top, then.' Samuel indicated the seat next to Jeremiah and then entered the coach. They set off for home.

Jeremiah grinned at his new companion. 'Bet you didn't think today would turn out like this.'

'No. I did not.' Relief flooded through Jed as he lifted his face to the sunshine and revelled in the fresh air and freedom so nearly lost to him forever. He would never forget the feeling in the pit of his stomach as the door of the cell had closed on him and the key scraped in the lock.

The look on his mother's face as he walked in through the door was one that Jed remembered for the rest of his life. She leapt to her feet, joy banished all weariness and she held her son tight. Tears welled in her eyes as she asked 'Why did the squire have you released, Jed?'

For once Jed could only say the truth. 'I don't know.'

Sarah was proud of her husband's actions but as he had predicted, others were not. Sunday came and after the church service James Hole took him aside. 'What in heaven's name persuaded you to do it?' he asked incredulously. 'We'll get him sooner or later, you know. What that boy needs is punishment and you'll regret your actions.' Before Samuel could reply he carried on. 'Now, speaking of your misplaced social conscience, there's someone I would like you to meet. Come to the house on Thursday evening. A gentlemen's dinner. You won't be disappointed.'

The guest of honour at the Manor that Thursday turned out to be the Rev. Becher of Southwell. Samuel had vaguely heard of him but was unaware that he was making a detailed report on the anti-pauper system. Seated next to him, Samuel very soon became engrossed in the subject of paupers and a lively exchange of opinions ensued.

'Outside relief is too open to abuse.' the Reverend said. If they are in employment and the wage paid is too small to feed the family, they are eligible for poor rate funds. Employers should pay the rate for the job and not expect the shortfall to be made up. If they are destitute and not in employment, then why should they be paid to do nothing? It encourages dependency and laziness.'

'But what alternative can you have?' replied Samuel. 'All who are willing to work are not always able to find it. As a civilised society we cannot condone abject poverty in our midst. We must care for those unable to care for themselves.'

James Hole hailed Rev. Becher from the end of the table. 'Did I not tell you I had found a suitable candidate for your committee?'

'The alternative, Samuel' the Reverend continued 'is the workhouse. A purpose built place of employment. Our new project at Southwell is almost complete and ready for the first in-mates. Everyone will work and everyone will receive basic shelter and enough food to sustain life. There will be rules and regulations and it will not be easy. At all costs we must encourage paupers to fend for themselves. It will be an alternative to the gutter. All the local parishes will be eligible to send the distressed there rather than pay for outside relief.'

The conversation continued late into the evening. Samuel became fired up with enthusiasm for his new found social awareness and promised to attend regular meetings at Southwell. He truly felt that this was something to which he could contribute and even perhaps change.

It was a few nights later that there was an insistent thumping on the front door of Beesthorpe Hall. McCready was on the point of retiring but with the oil lamp held high, he opened the door. To his great surprise, there stood Jed, red faced and breathing heavily, holding on tight to a struggling youth.

'Fetch the squire straightaway. I need to speak to him.'

'Mr. Bristowe has retired. What is it that can't wait?'

'This!' said Jed, holding up a dead rabbit.

'What is it? What's going on?' Samuel came down the stairs and looked in astonishment at the ragged visitors on the doorstep.

'He did this.' Jed said fiercely. 'Not me. You said I'd be responsible – well that ain't fair. No point me staying home if he does the poaching and I get the blame.' The youth struggled and began to protest. Jed tightened his grip. 'I knew he was up to something and I followed him. With my own eyes I saw him take it out of the trap and wring its neck.'

Samuel ran his hand wearily over his forehead. 'Very well, Jed. I believe you. Give the rabbit to McCready. You. What is your name?'

The youth gave his name. 'I shall call tomorrow and speak with your father. This will be your last warning. Now go home. Both of you.'

The next morning, Samuel rode out early. He called on the boy's father and told him there would be no reprieve if it happened again. 'Game laws are very harsh but what happens to your son if he is found guilty will not be my responsibility.'

Samuel rode on to the Smith's cottage. Suspicious, dark eyed children clustered around the door. 'Please ask your brother, Jed, to come out.'

Jed shooed the children aside and stood by the doorway, fearing the worst.

'Jed, I realise the position in which I have put you may be difficult – not just with my estate but with the others as well. I should like to ask you to come to work for me, as gamekeeper of the Beesthorpe estate. There's a little house in the woods. It needs repairing and a lot of work but you could make something of it. And I'll pay ten shillings a week. What do you say?'

Jed was speechless. He stared at the squire and nodded his head slowly.

'Right. Report to the kitchen as soon as you like and McCready will show you where the house is.'

'I know where it is.' Jed found his voice at last.

'Oh yes.' Samuel smiled. 'Of course you do.'

CHAPTER FIVE
Kitty

KITTY Wilkinson stared out across the muddy brown fields of Knapthorpe. It was late March and still winter refused to release its hold. The fat buds of the horse chestnuts waited, tightly closed against the bitter wind and the driving rain. The oncoming sky, heavy and threatening, showed no sign of relenting for the rest of the day. From her window, high up in Knapthorpe Manor, Kitty should have been able to see the towers of Southwell Minster but not today.

She was reluctant to leave her room and sat on her bed, idly twirling a lock of blond hair between her fingers. Solitary peace was something she had rarely experienced since coming into service but now everything had changed. The farm was abandoned and the house silent. Herbert Duffield was a broken man. He had come to realise all too late that the farm meant more to him than his extravagant wife and daughters. For years he had been behind with the rent whilst household expenses, born of the easy years of high wheat prices, slowly crippled his finances. Finally, the Duke of Rutland lost patience and a notice to quit was served. With bitter recriminations the wife and daughters had left, seeking refuge with relatives. The Duke's men drove away the stock and Herbert Duffield had stood alone in his silent yard. The servants watched. They had been given one week to remain in the house.

'What now?' Kitty thought as the rain beat harder against the windows and the landscape became obliterated in heavy cloud. She decided that on market day she would walk into Newark to look for work. One of the milking maids had recently found work in a tavern easily enough. Kitty left her room and wandered through the empty house. She felt no sympathy for the family. The six years she had been in service here had been hard. She had received nothing but a bed on which to lay after a meagre supper and a day's hard toil. The bleak house, stripped of its furniture and expensive drapes, sent Kitty's footsteps echoing through the empty rooms.

Putting on a cape and with a shawl over her head, Kitty went out into the rain. For some reason she felt compelled to go to the cottage. The overgrown hawthornes, bordering the narrow lane, afforded some protection from the wind and she trudged through the mud, on towards the tumbledown dwelling. It was empty, of course, as it had been since the day she had left, the day of aunt Esther's funeral.

How odd it was to see the house like this, so cold and bare amid the winter trees. In her memory, it had always been warm and sunny, set enchantingly amongst glorious summer trees in full, enticing foliage – not these sinister, skeletal boughs reaching out to scratch the windows. She pressed the latch and pushed on the door. Last autumn's leaves littered the floor, blown in through the broken windows. The remnants of a bird's nest lay scattered around the hearth. She remembered the day she had arrived – a little girl of ten, frightened and alone and unaware that she would spend three of the happiest years of her life here, under the loving protection of her aunt.

Kitty's hurried departure from Nottingham had been amid fear, panic and death. Fever had ravaged the district in which she lived with her parents and many had been carried away on carts from the squalid houses. Constant rain had reduced the narrow alley between the back to back houses to a stinking stream as the contents of the earth closets flooded over. Her father's tiny shoemakers shop had closed for business and her mother had sat at her dressmaker's table, anxiously peering into the street, day after day. On the morning that her father awoke with the fever, she urged Kitty to dress quickly. From the doorway, the child had bid her father goodbye and he had managed to smile and raise his hand.

'It won't be for long.' her mother had said as they picked their way out of the disease ridden alley and hurried along the street. 'Your aunt Esther will be so pleased to see you and you can return as soon as the sickness has gone.'

At the carrier's yard her mother had pulled the purse from her pocket and the coins jingled out into her hand. 'For you to take the child to a village beyond Southwell.' she said, thrusting the money towards the carrier.

The man shook his head. 'Carts all out today. Taking the dead.'

'No. Not a cart used for the sick.'

'Ain't no other, Missus.'

Her mother shook her head and thought. 'No cart. You have a horse available? My daughter can ride behind. She's very light.' An edge of desperation showed in her voice. She reached into her pocket once more and brought out a shiny sovereign. 'For you, if you take her. Now.'

The man nodded.

Kitty knew how hard-earned the precious money was. Her mother often sewed late into the night until her fingers bled and her eyes became weak and tired. She began to cry. 'I don't want to go, Mama. I'll stay and help.'

Her mother hugged her close and fought back her own tears. 'Your aunt will look after you. Remember your father and I love you very much and we shall come for you as soon as we can.'

Kitty held tight to the man's coat as the horse plodded down the street. Her mother stood and watched until they were out of sight and then hurried home to care for her husband.

The journey to Knapthorpe had taken the whole of the day. Kitty was cold, stiff and hungry when they finally arrived. 'Can you tell me where Esther Taylor might live?' the man asked a labourer. He pointed to a lane.

It was not with great pleasure that aunt Esther welcomed her niece. She listened to the man's story with hard eyes and pursed lips. Kitty hadn't liked the look of her at all. She was older than her mother, not so pretty and her clothes were rough and dirty. Never having had children of her own, aunt Esther felt uncomfortable in the presence of this beautiful child of her sister. Looking down at the blue eyes and golden hair, she felt old and ugly and her manner became gruff. 'You have your mother's hair. Everyone always loved her for her hair.' The words were heavy with resentment. 'Blond curls and a pretty face is all a man sees. No hope for the rest of us.'

Somehow, the first few days passed by in a series of questions and orders. Kitty was quick to learn and eager to help and gradually aunt Esther realised that this child, imposed as she had been upon her, was making her life easier and less lonely. She had been a widow for two years now and had reluctantly been allowed to stay on at the small farm her husband had rented on the Duke of Rutland's estate. She worked hard to keep her few cows and pigs.

Kitty watched as aunt Esther sat on the milking stool and with her head bent low into the side of the cow, expertly ran her fingers over the teats until the milk spurted into the bucket. She loved to turn the butter churn and hunt for eggs. Although she missed her parents, life on the farm settled into a happy routine. No word came from Nottingham.

One morning aunt Esther announced that she was going to see if she could find news of her sister. Kitty

44

walked to the end of the lane with her and watched as the farm cart disappeared over the hill. It was well after dark when she returned. She let herself into the cottage and Kitty jumped up in anticipation of the news she might have. Aunt Esther's face spoke for her. Eventually, she said 'I couldn't find your parents, child. The fever took them both. I'm sorry.'

Kitty sat still, weighed down by the finality, the realisation that she would never see her parents again. She had been cut off forever from her previous life.

' The landlord took everything in lieu of rent. There's nothing left. You will stay with me, now. We'll look after each other.' The words were delivered flat, devoid of emotion, but Kitty could see the tears in her aunt's eyes. They hugged each other and mourned together. Gradually, over a period of time, a solid bond developed between the two and contented months turned into happy years.

Kitty lacked for nothing and blossomed under her aunt's care. Summers were colourful and vivid, with carefree days spent picking wild flowers and laying in the long grass, watching dragonflies hover over the dew ponds. In autumn they roamed the lanes picking blackberries, mushrooms from the fields and apples from the orchard. The freezing days of winter brought painful hands and feet as they tended the animals, but every evening aunt and niece sat companionably by a dancing fireside. They took turns to read aloud, holding the pages close to a flickering candle, peering into the dim light. Aunt Esther told stories – Bible stories, fairy stories and folk stories. From their fireside they escaped into a magical fantasy world, every evening before bedtime.

One morning, it was obvious that aunt Esther was ill. As the weeks passed by she took to her bed more frequently and left the full brunt of the chores to Kitty.

'Nothing to worry about.' she'd say as Kitty's anxious face leaned over her. 'Just a mite worn out, is all. As soon as I've had my rest, I'll be chasing you about, you'll see.' Following aunt Esther's instructions, Kitty did her best and brought to the bedside a bowl of broth. 'Not bad. Not bad at all for a first attempt.' The aunt's eyes rested on the girl as she sipped the hot liquid. 'What would I have done if my sister had not sent you to me, Kitty? I can't imagine life without you now.'

Despite Kitty's best nursing efforts, aunt Esther grew thinner. Her once strong face became gaunt and her body shrivelled. In gruesome timing, the pigs took ill with swine fever and the cows went dry.

'Go to farmer Duffield. Ask him if he would be so good as to pay me a visit.'

Kitty went up to the big house. Mr. Duffield listened to the young girl and nodded. 'Tell your aunt I'll be along this afternoon.'

The big man removed his hat as he stepped through the low door and into aunt Esther's cottage. His boots banged heavily on the bare boards of the winding staircase and he stood at the end of her bed. He knew at once that she was dying.

'It's sorry I am to see you taken so sick, Esther.' he said.

'My concerns are not for myself but for my niece.' Her voice was weak but her manner as forthright as ever. 'You'll know we've lost stock lately and I can do nothing now. What you may not know is that I am in debt with the farm rent. I owe a whole year's worth and no hope of paying now.' She sighed heavily. 'So much for letting a poor widow carry on the farm after her husband is taken. I managed for a while, though. You know that.'

Kitty stood in the doorway. She hadn't been dismissed and she knew that although this was business talk, it may concern her.

46

'They'll be taking all they can in lieu of rent.' Aunt Esther continued. 'I suppose you'll get my meadows now. You've always wanted them. Good grass – and buttercups.' A rueful smile temporarily lightened the solemnity of the words. 'But what will happen to the child? She has no-one but me. Will you take her in? She works hard. I've taught her that.'

Mr. Duffield turned to look upon Kitty. She stared back at him from the doorway. He nodded towards the sick woman. 'I'll see her right, Esther. You can be sure of that. Rest easy now.'

From that day, the confidences grew more intimate. Kitty learned a great deal about her mother's and aunt Ester's early life, growing up in Nottingham, the daughters of a modest but respectable tradesman. She would sit at the end of the bed. Her aunt would begin to talk and out it would all tumble. Sometimes she thought aunt Esther had forgotten that she was even there.

'And then I fell in love. Hah. Head over heels in love with a wonderful boy. We walked out together. He was an apprentice cobbler.' For a while her pained face became transformed with the warm memory and then returned to bitterness. 'And then he fell in love with your mother. She was so very much prettier, you see. All the young men were captivated by her. I was broken hearted when they married.'

Aunt Esther stopped to look fully at Kitty. 'Your parents were very happy together and that made me even more unhappy, if you can understand. I married the first man who came along, just to get away from them. Not that Mr. Taylor wasn't a good man – he was, for sure and I did grow to love him in my way. But what I felt for your father was an emotion so strong.'

Kitty swallowed hard and felt uncomfortable to hear these intimate secrets. Sensing this, aunt Esther laid a hand on her arm. 'At one time I thought I hated your

47

mother because she stole something so precious from me. But I don't hate her now. I'm so grateful to her for sending you to me, Kitty.' Her calloused, hardworking hand reached out and enfolded Kitty's small, soft one. 'The years since you arrived here that night, so unexpectedly, have been the happiest of my life. It's so important that you know these things, my love. For when I'm gone. So important.'

Aunt Esther died a few weeks later. The scent of lilac blossom filled the air as the farm labourers carried the coffin from the cottage. It was loaded onto a cart and taken up the grassy lane and on to Caunton churchyard for burial.

For Kitty, the sunshine years were over. She went into service at Knapthorpe Manor. Any hopes that aunt Esther may have harboured concerning her welfare in the household, did not come about. Kitty was a servant and for the next five years was treated without favour or even kindness. Herbert Duffield gave no thought to his promise to the dying woman. He was disinterested in domestic affairs and his wife's rise in the social scene was her only concern. Miserable years passed by in a grey haze of domestic toil.

All these memories crowded in on Kitty as she stood in the derelict cottage where she had been so happy. It didn't seem possible. Soon she would be gone from Knapthorpe for good. Nothing to hold on to now – just faded images of a previous life. She shivered as a blast of icy wind funnelled through the broken window panes. Kitty took one last look around, turned and pulled the door closed behind her.

CHAPTER SIX
Decisions

A S Jeremiah saddled up, Henry stamped and snorted excitably in anticipation of the gallop. As a carriage horse, he was constrained by the traces, metering out his energies in a restricted manner. However high stepping and headstrong the pair became, their pace was still a trot, at best a canter. But when riding out, Samuel gave Henry his head and he pounded along the fields and lanes, his hooves biting deep into the earth, sending clods and stones flying.

The charged power of the horse transferred itself to the rider and Samuel felt energised with exhilaration. He rode down through the park and crossed the beck via the cutting. The carriage road stretched up through Lockabeck meadow and on past Readyfield farm. Samuel galloped on, through master's beck furlong and Mather wood and finally reined in on a ridge overlooking the next valley. Startled woodcock flew up and pheasants screeched off in alarm as Samuel looked down on the Winkburn estate which stretched out before him. The magnificent mansion with the old church nestling beside it was the focus of the village and a handful of cottages set amongst the elms and beeches completed the scene. Samuel urged Henry into a gentle canter down to Winkburn Hall.

As the horse was led away by a groom, Col. Burnell greeted his guest and escorted him into the house. Samuel's new riding coat was stiff and his boots too shiny compared to Col. Burnell's comfortable attire, which looked as though it had been moulded on to him over a period of years. He was a countryman. He lived for his farms as well as hunting and shooting. His well worn boots reflected his pursuits and his expensive jacket sagged and creased accordingly. Hunting dogs congregated in the hallway, eagerly watching their master for a signal to send them into a frenzy of activity.

'Lie down.' They slunk to the floor.

'Come and take wine with your neighbour, Samuel and then I shall show you the estate.'

The view from the great windows was so expansive that Samuel was moved to exclaim 'Surely we can see most of it from here!'

'Ah, yes. All you can see in this direction and and then back as far as Maplebeck the other way. The land is mixed. Some of it is heavy in parts and causes the farmers many problems when it becomes waterlogged. Quite unworkable. When the wheat prices were high, everyone wanted to grow it, but the land isn't always suitable. Won't have it. We have taken two farms in hand just this week.'

'In hand?' asked Samuel, feeling that this was something he should know.

'When prices fall and tenants can't pay the rent, they quit the farm – often owing money. It's hard to find another tenant to take it on. So the home farm agrees to take it in hand – to manage it, graze it, save it from ruin until a new tenant can be found.'

Samuel sighed in exasperation. 'Why is there so much inefficiency and complacency? Can nothing be done to save these people from misery and debt?'

Col. Burnell frowned and strode to the window. With his hands clasped firmly behind his back he turned on Samuel. 'Well now. I know you are an impulsive and indeed fortunate young man but you must understand that agriculture fluctuates. Fortunes are made and lost. Complacency must not be confused with acceptance of facts.'

'I would make many changes if it were in my power.' Samuel said.

Col. Burnell turned. 'If you are serious about making changes, and have the energy and resources to do it, you can.' Samuel looked at him sceptically. 'There is to be an election soon. Stand for parliament. Show your passion to the electorate. Use their vote to empower these changes of which you speak. Think on that, Samuel Bristowe. Turn your words into actions. Now I'll show you the estate.'

Samuel followed his host out into fresh March winds. They cantered off down the road to view the farms. Heavy clouds threatened, and then blew over, saving their raindrops to deposit further down the valley. The grass fields had not yet greened over, the weather being too cold to promote any new spring shoots. Cattle and sheep huddled by barn doorways, hoping to be fed the last few meagre whisps of winter feed. From Dilliner Farm they cut back through the woods towards Hockerton.

'This is Knapthorpe Manor.' said Col. Burnell, indicating the farm ahead. 'We have it in hand.' The horses had slowed to a walk. There was an air of desolation about the place. The solid house was perched on high ground and a keen wind whistled around its walls. 'This poor chap was more set on social climbing than paying attention to his bills. Failed to learn his lesson in time. Lost the lot.'

A servant girl crossed the road ahead of them. Col. Burnell continued. 'The servants have until the end of the week to leave. I expect they will find work of some kind in Newark.'

Samuel thought quickly. 'I think I may need an extra hand at Beesthorpe. My housekeeper is stretched to the limit.' he said.

'Well, there's your opportunity. Hey, you girl!'

51

The girl spun round and the shawl slipped from her head, revealing a mass of blond hair. She stood still as the horses came right up to her.

'Do you have a position to go to?' Col. Burnell asked.

'No Sir. Not yet, Sir.'

'It may be' said Samuel 'that I could offer you a job at Beesthorpe. Come to the Hall tomorrow morning and we shall see. What is your name?'

'Kitty Wilkinson, Sir.'

The next morning, Kitty threaded her way through the lanes and tracks on the shortest route to Beesthorpe. She passed by Earlshaw Farm and waved to Ann Cheetham as she trudged across the yard to the cow stall. The farm was in a dip and in wet times the surface water ran down through the new house. The frame of the original farmhouse still stood, just, within the confines of a flooded moat and it was still possible to see that it had been a very fine house indeed. It was always wet here. Kitty was hard put to find a reasonable route through the rain-filled ruts. She lifted her skirt high so as not to have the hem covered in mud.

As she reached the top of the last hill, she stopped to wipe her boots on the grass, and there was Beesthorpe Hall standing proudly in the valley. It looked friendly and warm. She reached the carriage road and skipped across the stepping stones over the beck, stopping in the middle to scoop up the clear water to wash her hands and face and the last traces of mud from her boots. In the meadow vivid clumps of celandines shone golden in the sunshine and on the bank primroses peeped through the undergrowth. Kitty's spirits lifted.

Self consciously, she stood before Sarah in the morning room, answering her questions as best she could. Kitty thought the young mistress had a sickly look about her, but she was kind and treated her with respect.

'I understand' said Sarah 'that the farmer left without giving references but Col. Burnell has vouched for you. We require a hard working girl here. Do you think you would be able to manage the heavy work that goes with the duties of a laundry maid and housemaid?'

Kitty looked up at her new employer. 'Oh yes, Ma'am. I know how to work hard.'

That evening, as they prepared for bed, Sarah told her husband that she had lost the child she had been carrying. Samuel held her close and comforted her. He was lost for words and certainly could not now divulge the news he had been harbouring. He had made the decision, after listening to the forthright words of Col. Burnell, to go into politics. If he was to achieve any personal standing it had to be through his own efforts. His mind had almost been made up when he saw the servant girl. The house must be well run, dinners hosted, and attended. He would need his wife's support and he was sure he would have it. As soon as Sarah was well, he would break the news to her.

CHAPTER SEVEN
McCready

WHEN Samuel Bristowe rang the bell which sounded in the servants hall, McCready made his way through the house to the drawing room and stood quietly before him. Samuel put down his newspaper and asked directly 'Have you settled in your role of butler here, McCready?'

The unexpected question, taking him by surprise, brought a genuine response. 'Most certainly, Sir.'

Good. I'm glad to hear it because I have plans which will involve more organisation within the household. Entertaining and such.' He rose and stood by the fireplace as though to give his announcement more authority. 'Politics, McCready. I intend to stand for election.'

'The household will do all it can in your support, Sir.'

'The new housemaid will, I am sure, make the workload easier but it is imperative that high standards are achieved and maintained.'

'Yes, indeed, Sir.'

'Walking back to the kitchen McCready stood for a moment and gazed out of the window overlooking the parkland. The distant sails of the mill moved slowly against the blue sky and McCready felt very content with his life here at Beesthorpe.

So he was totally unprepared for the feelings of turmoil which crowded in on him as he looked down at Kitty Wilkinson, the new laundry maid. It was odd because he was quite unused to feelings of any kind evoked by the opposite sex. As a gauche young man he had pursued the local girls with as much enthusiasm as any, but somehow they unfailingly sought to ridicule and demoralize him. Perhaps it was his unusual, ungainly height, his gaunt face with the bad skin or, of course, his habit of staring and his painful shyness. Whatever the reason, the girls regarded him as freakish and treated him heartlessly with their giggling, sniggering and taunting.

Life in service at Twyford Hall had not been easy after Lizzie, the love of his young life. Everyone on the estate knew that he had fallen for her and it had amused her to lead him on, right up to when he asked her to marry him. Her reaction to the proposal was to take offence at his presumption and she rebuffed him. His inability to understand the reason for her displeasure irritated her beyond words and she began to loathe him and take every opportunity to belittle him. He was deeply hurt, his passion recoiled within him and he retreated in on himself. Always awkward of speech, he became diffident and succeeded in building a wall around his feelings, determined never to have them so cruelly used again.

By the time he came to Beesthorpe it could be said that McCready had 'grown into himself'. Now in his thirties, his body and face had filled out with maturity, so his presence was no longer alarming. Being economic with words, his influence was usually to calm and reassure. His quiet manner concealed the void he felt within himself but many times he reflected that if he were to find happiness anywhere, it would be at Beesthorpe.

'If you please, Sir, Mrs. Welby said I was to report to you.'

John McCready looked down at Kitty Wilkinson and was unable to utter one word. His silence made her fidget. She looked at him, then away, then at her feet. Should she keep talking? Why didn't he speak? Was he angry with her for something she'd done?' Her round, blue eyes were puzzled as she glanced back at him. She had no way of knowing that he was spellbound, completely smitten.

Finally, McCready cleared his throat and managed 'You will assist Mrs. Welby with the washing and house cleaning duties and be an extra hand for her when Mr. & Mrs. Bristowe entertain.' He turned abruptly and strode off down the gloomy servants' corridor.

With the uneasy feeling that she had offended, Kitty went back to the kitchen.

'Nothing to worry about, dear ' Mrs. Welby assured her 'He's a fair man but he just doesn't speak much. A bit awkward with people. You'll get used to it. Now, I'll show you how to fill the copper.'

Days passed before McCready could muster enough courage to speak directly to Kitty. He expected her alarming impact on him to wane at any time but it didn't. It grew more painful. With her wellbeing at heart, he started finding ways of making life easier for her. Coming into the wash-house one day, he saw her wrestling with yards of table and bed linen. She was beating the suds through and then heaving the weighty material up to the mangle and using all her strength to turn the handle. Her wet hair was stuck to her forehead, her cheeks were red and glistening and her hands and arms red raw with the hot water and the exertion. She still looked beautiful to him.

'Dear girl, you look exhausted! Let me carry the basket out to the garden for you.' Kitty stared in amazement. She straightened her back and lifted up her forearm to brush back the wet curls clinging to the side of her face. She smiled at him warmly. McCready's concern was odd and she didn't know quite how to react. This was her job and, although it was tiring, she quite enjoyed it.

He picked up the basket of heavy wet washing and set off to the orchard. He felt elated. At last, a way of showing his feeling for her. She was bound to be grateful for his concern.

'Thank you Mr. McCready. You are most kind.'

Encouraged at last, McCready began to find other little ways of easing Kitty's load. Mrs. Welby was quick to notice the change, and the reason for it, and spoke frankly to Kitty. 'I think Mr. McCready is well taken with you, my girl. I never seen him so at ease and considerate.'

It was a fact that had not been lost on Kitty either, but hearing confirmation from Mrs. Welby gave her confidence. From then on, as McCready became bold enough to be in her presence and speak directly to her, Kitty responded with flirtatious eyes and ever more dazzling smiles. When her work was not attended to in the proper way, he readily overlooked it. This was becoming the easiest place of service that Kitty could imagine and she took more and more liberties. She began to indulge in a familiarity above her domestic station, confident in her ability to keep McCready's support for her. He revelled in her attention to his needs and his heart swelled with foolish pride when she went out of her way to bestowe the most simple favours on him. She would solicitously serve the evening meal to him and then run to fetch his pipe and tobacco that he might enjoy his customary evening smoke. She was well aware that he was quietly watching her as she washed the dishes and put the kitchen in order.

One day, silently approaching the kitchen, he heard Kitty talking to Mrs. Welby. Just for the pleasure of hearing her voice, he stood with his head bent, listening at the door. He started as he heard his name mentioned. 'I think Mr. McCready has gentle eyes. Don't you think he has kind, gentle eyes?' McCready's heart soared and his eyes did indeed become soft and gentle. His affection for this lovely girl was becoming stronger by the day but he was acutely aware of the age difference between them. He was anxious not to frighten her off and decided to advance his suit unmistakably but slowly. He would take the time to win her.

CHAPTER EIGHT
Jeremiah

SUNDAY afternoons offered a small but welcome change in the routine of the servants. Mr. & Mrs. Bristowe attended the church of St. Andrew in Caunton for the morning service. The carriage was brought around to the front of the house at ten thirty by Jeremiah Jennings, the young coachman. Jeremiah was an extraordinarily skilled horseman. Despite his short stature, he exercised his will over the powerful animals with a dominance they respected. He rarely cracked the whip but communicated through the reins. He used his masterful voice to command and to soothe and after gaining their confidence, there was nothing the horses wouldn't do for him. It was much the same with girls.

Jeremiah was a good looking young man with a mop of floppy brown hair like a horse's mane. He was never at a loss for words, witty remarks seeming to spill from him effortlessly and girls adored him. From the first moment he had observed Kitty from the stable courtyard he had been intrigued. She had ignored him. She had turned her pretty face away and flounced her golden curls in a display of disinterest. It was to Jeremiah's great annoyance that, since Kitty had joined the household, Samuel Bristowe had constantly required his services from early morning to late evening, back and forth to political meetings in Newark. He had had no chance to engage her in conversation, turn on the full power of his charm and thereby notch up another conquest.

Sunday morning service was attended by the heads of households. Servants spent the morning peeling and scraping, cooking and serving. The Sunday luncheon was a social affair with villagers visiting and the vicar taking his pick of the best invitation available. The afternoon then presented itself for a brief respite from the domestic chores. Jenny Cocking set off to walk to Kersall and Mrs. Welby and Kitty put on their bonnets and prepared to walk down to Caunton for the afternoon church service. McCready accompanied them. With his black top hat giving him even more height, his six foot frame was in startling contrast to the two women and he towered over them. Kitty and Mrs. Welby got on well together but the elder lady was acutely aware of the tensions brought about by Kitty's arrival and her inappropriate behaviour towards McCready. She had tried to warn her. What the outcome of it all would be she couldn't imagine. They proceeded down the drive together in an awkward silence.

McCready eventually fell into step beside Kitty as best he could with his long legs. He attempted light conversation but his habit of making the most mundane remark seem serious and threatening was a handicap to them both. Kitty did her best, making herself extremely agreeable and soon they reached the edge of the village. The church bells began to summon them to the service. The dirt road meandered on past thatched cottages as well as the Manor, the splendid home of Mr. & Mrs. Hole. They crossed the footbridge over the beck but as they reached the church gate there was a shout behind them and they turned to see Jeremiah panting up the road, dodging chickens and church-goers, red faced from having run all the way.

'You were nearly too late, Jeremiah.' said Mrs. Welby, her suspicions aroused as to the real reason for the haste.

McCready gave him a black look. Kitty, behind McCready's back, turned her head to one side, raised her blue eyes and flashed him a coquettish glance.

Jeremiah was glad he had run so fast. However, his attempts to try to sit next to Kitty came to nothing as

McCready seemed glued to her side. They were squashed up tight together in the pew and Kitty, seated between Mrs. Welby and McCready, looked straight ahead. They sang the hymns, said the prayers, listened to the sermon and emerged into the late afternoon sunshine.

Mrs. Welby eased Kitty to one side to introduce her to one or two friends but as they followed the path between the gravestones it was McCready's dark form that constantly shadowed her. Jeremiah finally grew tired of trying to outmanoeuvre him and sloped off to enjoy the company of a couple of girls he knew.

That evening, Jeremiah was able to join the rest of the servants for supper in the kitchen. For once his services were not required. The coach was in the coach house, the horses in their own stable and Mr. & Mrs. Bristowe were enjoying an evening at home together. In the kitchen Jeremiah was happy with the seating arrangement, as McCready took his place at the customary head of table position. The young coachman chatted away as Kitty laid the table and Mrs. Welby put the food out – cold mutton and pickled cabbage. McCready silently carved the meat. Jeremiah talked throughout the meal, mostly addressing Mrs. Welby, and Kitty was careful not to appear too interested or laugh too much at his joking. He had seated himself next to her and she was acutely aware of his nearness. She took in every detail of his leather boots and dark green jacket with the gold braiding. Her eyes were constantly drawn to his rough hands and she breathed in the smell of horses that exuded from him.

McCready didn't like Jeremiah and the reason was obvious. He was in every single way, the exact opposite from him. The young coachman's easy-going, light hearted manner was a delight to all he met, whereas the butler compared badly – so constrained by his stiff, unnatural speech and tendency to glower.

Kitty was careful not to show her enjoyment of Jeremiah's company but she loved every minute of it. He embarked on stories of recent events in Newark. Forced to spend much time there recently, he seemed to be at the centre of events and his colourful observations of the political goings-on painted a new picture to Kitty, who knew nothing whatever of politics. She couldn't wait for her first day off.

Every fourth Sunday Kitty was allowed off from ten o'clock in the morning until six o'clock at night. When the day arrived she hurried through her morning tasks and changed from her servant's uniform into her own skirt and shawl. She raced all the way down the long drive anxious not to miss the carrier's cart into Newark. She had told Mrs. Welby that she was going to see her friend at the Wing Tavern, which indeed she was, but who knew what else the day might bring?

As usual, the occupants of the open waggon had to squeeze themselves into a small space on the bench with baskets and sacks at their feet. The chatter was of barter – the price of eggs and butter, how much they had sold last week and how much they hoped it would be next. Kitty pulled her shawl tighter to her as a breeze blew up and the horses trotted on down the road, eating up the distance to Newark. They crossed the bridge over the river Trent at the village of Kelham and then again at the entrance to the market town as the ruin of the medieval castle came into view. It was a place for vagrants and large numbers of homeless poor lived in the shacks erected alongside the crumbling and half destroyed walls. Tenements had grown up beside the once magnificent gatehouse, reducing the area to little more than a slum. Kitty never liked the look of it. They continued up Beastmarket Hill but being Sunday, there was no cattle market.

The town was a jumble of narrow streets and lanes. Old houses crowded in on each other, barely leaving enough space for a cart to pass between. Kitty walked along Bar Gate, past rows of cottages, and turned right into Kirk Gate. St. Mary's parish church dominated from the end of the street with its majestic spire reaching up to the sky and its great oak door. Half timbered houses and shops leaned out towards each other into the narrow street. A shout went up and before it had turned the corner, Kitty heard the clatter of the horses hooves and the wheels on the cobbles announcing the arrival of the London mail coach. It bore down on her and she was forced to leap to the side. Instantly there was a flurry of activity. The doors of the Kings Arms and the Boar's Head opened and the landlords were on the street welcoming one and all with the promise of good beer and lodgings. The horses stamped to a halt, their sweated flanks heaving. The coach continued creaking as people spilled down from on top of it as well as inside. Everyone looked weary, stiff and travel-worn. As Kitty walked by, the horses were already snorting their relief and the steam was rising from their backs like a cloud.

Skirting past the church, Kitty came to the Wing Tavern where she found her friend, Mary, working as she did every day, taking jugs of beer to the tables and washing the tankards in a bucket of dirty water out in the backyard. Mary was pleased to see her and the girls chatted happily. Something was going on in the market place though, and Kitty's attention was distracted.

'It's another political speech, I expect.' Mary said dismissively.

Kitty remembered Jeremiah's lively stories and although she was not at all interested in politics, felt compelled to go and join the crowds to see what was happening. The market place was thronging with people of all sorts. The usual pedlars were there, carrying their wares on their backs, and traders had pitched up their handcarts and were doing some trade, but there were other sections of society too. Groups of men stood around, waiting. Some were ragged, low class working men. Others were gentlemen in high hats, breeches and leather boots. Some were accompanied by smartly dressed ladies with pretty bonnets and parasols. Kitty threaded her way between them all, listening to snatches of conversation. Suddenly, from behind, her hand was seized and she was spun around. She gasped in alarm and found herself staring into the laughing eyes of Jeremiah.

'I've been looking for you. I knew you'd come.' he said with a wide grin.

Kitty was torn between indignation and pleasure. Finally, she smiled and they both laughed together.

'Did you know Mr. Bristowe is going to speak this afternoon? It's going to be a very important speech for Newark. I've heard them all talking. Going to give the Duke of Newcastle a run for his money. You must stay to hear it.' Jeremiah rushed on proudly.

'I have to catch the cart back at five o-clock. When will it start?' Kitty's few precious hours of freedom seemed to be flashing by.

'About four I think, so you'll be alright. Come with me now, though. I have to get back to the horses. Mr. Bristowe will be coming to the steps of the town hall in the carriage.'

Kitty was dragged along through the crowds, holding tight to Jeremiah's hand. Suddenly he stopped by a pedlar holding a tray of haberdashery. Laid out neatly were coloured ribbons. On impulse Jeremiah turned to Kitty and said 'When I was looking for you – it was your hair I was remembering. I kept looking for your hair. It's the colour of corn.' He felt awkward and for once, the words didn't come quite so easily.

The pedlar, sensing a sale, wasted no time. 'Ribbon for the lady, is it?'

Jeremiah selected two red ribbons and handed over two pennies. With a serious expression, he held the ribbons against Kitty's hair and then presented them to her. She looked at them with delight, her eyes rounder than ever. The tender moment passed and they dashed off again, cutting through a narrow archway into Chain Lane. Butchers and bakershops muddled together and ragged children spilled from doorways, playing in the lane and risking collision with the unsteady clients weaving out of the Kings Head. They crossed into Boar Lane and, dodging the heaps of steaming manure, arrived at the back entrance to the stableyard of the Ram Inn.

Samuel Bristowe's matching black horses were resting in the stables and Jeremiah spoke to them reassuringly as he wasted no time in tacking them up and backing them into the traces. They gave him no trouble. Kitty watched from the yard gateway, anxious not to get in the way.

Securing the last few buckles, Jeremiah was finally satisfied and ran his hands admiringly over the horses' flanks. Their coats shone like burnished coal.

'There. Now we're ready. They'll be coming out soon. We'll be driving round to the town hall so you go back to the market place to get a good view. I reckon if you stand somewhere near the bear baiting post you'll be able to hear alright.' Jeremiah's excitement was catching but before leaving Kitty took out the ribbons from her pocket and looked at them.

'Thank you. They are beautiful.'

A waiter came out of the Ram Inn and gestured to Jeremiah. 'Mr. Bristowe is ready now. Take the carriage round to the door.'

Jeremiah gave Kitty a wink and a cocky turn of his head as she ran off. He manoeuvred the carriage through the narrow entrance and out on to Castle Gate.

The crowds in the market place had grown thicker and it was with difficulty that Kitty squeezed herself into position near the town hall steps. People began craning their necks and the tension grew. Which way would the carriage come? Would they be able to see or hear? Excitement heightened as six outriders, each carrying a light blue flag, made their entrance near the Governors House. Men on foot carrying banners, gaily decorated with blue ribbons, marched behind and finally Mr. Bristowe's horses appeared, tossing their heads anxiously, as Jeremiah proudly guided them through the crowds. The carriage cover was down and inside, surrounded by blue ribbons sat Samuel Bristowe himself. Some of the crowd cheered. Kitty was thrilled.

Samuel Bristowe stood up in the carriage and lifted his hand for silence. The crowd settled.

'Gentlemen, I come among you today as one who would wish to solicit your vote, to represent you and your interests in Parliament.' His voice was strong and carried well and the crowd was attentive. ' I must assure you that my pecuniary circumstances, though sufficient to support myself and my family in the greatest of comfort, are insufficient to warrant my spending much on the present occasion. Nor would I ever sit in Parliament if I could only do so by purchasing the votes of those who would place me there – unlike my adversaries whose illiberality is only equalled by their corruption.'

A huge cheer went up from the working class men and clenched fists were raised in salutes of approval. The tall hats looked at each other and muttered. Heartened by the response, Samuel Bristowe continued, his voice growing louder and more confident.

'I pledge to you to release the people of Newark from bondage. Corrupt practices have been used which are discreditable in the extreme. Are not the charitable donations bequeathed for the benefit of the town in the hands of those, who at the election, deny you the inestimable privilege of giving, according to your wishes, an unbought vote?'

An even bigger cheer went up but a scuffle broke out in the crowd and Mr. Bristowe stopped speaking. A menacing group of rough men had surrounded a gathering of cheerers and angry voices raised in intimidation turned into fighting. Punches were traded and although the surrounding group were armed with staves and cudgels, they were quickly outnumbered as others came from all quarters of the market place to see them off.

'That's right, lads. You show the Duke of Newcastle's henchmen what we think! It's time we voted as we please.' Shouts of support went up all around Kitty. The volatile crowd surged forward to the carriage and she feared she would be trampled on the cobblestones. She tried to call to Jeremiah but his attention was fully on the horses. A rough hand rested on her shoulder and eased her to a more upright position.

'You stand in front of me, Miss.' A burly worker positioned himself to protect Kitty from the jostling crowd. Samuel Bristowe continued with his passionate speech, his voice filling the market place as his confidence grew. It was a dramatic scene. The carriage was framed by the classical columns of the town hall, a grandiose building which dominated the square. The black horses and blue Liberal flags stood out against the honey coloured stone and Samuel Bristowe became more and more impassioned. He spoke against the Corn Laws, the Game Laws and the wretched state of the Irish poor. The abolition of slavery and the emancipation of Roman Catholics received his passionate attention before he finally returned to the topic which incensed him the most – Freedom of Election.

'When hardworking men with families to feed, are bribed by their employer with the promise of free coal if

66

they vote for the Conservative member, what can be the purpose of an election? The prospect of being put out of a job and turned out of their house does not constitute a free vote. That those elected then go on to serve their own needs rather than those of their electors is scandalous!'

Roars of support came from some groups – silence from others. The air was heavy with tension. Kitty knew the time was passing by and she needed to get back to Castle Gate as the carrier's waggon would be leaving soon but it was impossible to move. Although the clock on the church struck five, she had no choice but to wait until the speech was over and the crowd had begun to disperse. Eventually, as Jeremiah eased the carriage through the mass of people, the movement allowed her to escape and she ran through the lanes as fast as she could. The cart had gone without her.

'Left nigh on ten minutes ago, Miss.' one of the stable boys informed her.

Kitty's face crumpled. There was nothing else for it. She would have to walk home to Caunton. The seven mile distance was not a problem to her but it would take some time and she would be late. If she was going to get away with this, she would have to be very nice indeed to Mr. McCready.

Kitty ran down Beastmarket Hill, partly because she needed to make all haste and partly so as not to be accosted by the vagrants. She crossed the bridge and took the dusty road to Kelham. Soon her shoes were dirty and her legs were tired but she hurried on. Dusk was starting to settle as she came to the long straight before Debdale Hill. Ahead of her loomed the prospect of Dark Turn. She tried to quicken her pace, fearful of being caught there alone in the dark.

Dark Turn was a section of road with a very bad reputation. After the hill, the road descended and eased to the right. It became very narrow with steep banks and high trees on either side which met together overhead, creating a tunnel, gloomy on even the sunniest of days. Within this tunnel the road made a sharp left turn. Any on-coming carriage or animal could not be seen until a collision was almost inevitable. And it was haunted. Local legend said that here lived a boggart – a ghost dog, and on encountering it, people had been known to die of fright.

Kitty's heart was beating fast and she was breathing hard as she started to run into Dark Turn. She must get through as quickly as possible. All she could hear was the thud of her shoes and her own laboured breathing. She developed a pain in her side but she couldn't stop to rest now. She had to keep running. She heard a sound behind her and stumbled on. Was it the ghost dog? There was nowhere to hide. The banks rose steeply from either side of the narrow road. The noise became louder. It was right behind her. She started to sob.

At the last possible moment, Jeremiah caught sight of the figure in the road ahead and hauled hard back on the reins 'Whoa. Whoa. Steady now.' The horses, forced to curb their pace so quickly, reared back on their haunches and squealed in alarm. Kitty whirled around to see the coach almost upon her and the horses' hooves towering over her head. She stood frozen to the spot, her terrified face showing white in the shadowy gloom.

'Kitty! Are you alright?' Jeremiah's voice called out to her but the frightened girl was unable to answer.

Samuel Bristowe opened the coach door and peered out anxiously. 'What is the problem, Jeremiah? Have we hurt someone?'

'No, Sir. It's Kitty Wilkinson. I didn't see her until we were almost upon her. She's only frightened, I think.'

'What are you doing out here at this time of night, girl? It's almost dark.'

Kitty still couldn't quite put her words together so Jeremiah answered for her.

'It was her afternoon off, Sir. She came into Newark to hear your speech and must have missed the carrier's cart home.'

Samuel Bristowe was feeling tired but pleased with the way the day had gone. He was not going to be cross with one of his servants for supporting him.

'Very well. She can ride home with us.'

'Come up here with me, Kitty.' Jeremiah said quickly as he reached out a hand to guide her up on the high seat.

Suddenly realising the good fortune of the moment, Kitty smiled in relief and, with her legs still trembling a little, she managed to find her way up to sit beside Jeremiah. They both sat smiling in the dark. Jeremiah encouraged the horses on and soon they were out of Dark Turn and heading towards Dean Hall. They faced the western sky and before their eyes it flared up in a deep shade of pink above layers of clouds in grey and blue.

'What did you think to it then? The speech, I mean.' Jeremiah asked. He liked having Kitty sitting next to him, their thighs touching.

'Oh, it was very exciting but a little frightening. I wasn't expecting a fight.'

Jeremiah grinned at her. Their eyes met and a bond forged itself between them. They had shared the experience of the momentous afternoon and both knew it was the beginning of a deep friendship. And now, to be riding home together, as if it was meant to be.

'Thank you for the ribbons.' Kitty whispered.

For once Jeremiah did not feel the need to come up with a cocky, witty reply. Taking both reins in the one hand, he reached out and held her hand tight in his. The horses knew their way home and trotted on towards the disappearing sunset.

It was with mixed feelings that John McCready greeted Kitty's belated arrival home. He had been worried, anxious that some misfortune had overtaken her but whilst he was relieved to see her on Mr. Bristowe's coach, he was also slightly irritated that she was sitting next to Jeremiah.

'No need to be cross with her for lateness, McCready.' Samuel Bristowe put the matter straight immediately. 'Kitty was at the market place. The meeting was a little boisterous and ran late. And' he added rather smugly 'I am pleased to say – it was a success.' He smiled and strode off to find his wife to relay the events of the day to her.

Kitty readily accepted McCready's offered hand to descend from the coach. 'It was very exciting Mr. McCready but a little frightening at times.' She looked deep into his eyes and held his hand a little longer than necessary.

'Hurry along now, Kitty. Mrs. Welby has supper ready.'

That night Kitty had difficulty in getting off to sleep. Although she was physically very tired, her emotions were heightened and she constantly re-lived the exciting moments of the day. She laid the red ribbons on the pillow beside her and hoped the gift had meant the same to Jeremiah as it did to her. She would remember sitting beside him high up on the coach for the rest of her life. Snuggling deep under the blankets and smiling content-edly, she finally fell into a satisfying sleep.

CHAPTER NINE

Fate

THERE was a tacit agreement between Kitty and Jeremiah that they would not make their attraction to each other obvious. It wasn't easy. Kitty knew that McCready liked her because she was pretty and she even thought he might be falling in love with her. Why else would he make life so easy for her? It made a pleasant change to be considered and cared for and she wasn't going to spoil that in a hurry. She decided that the more risks she took to see Jeremiah, however briefly, then the nicer she needed to be to Mr. McCready.

Life for Kitty took on the excitement of duplicity. She seemed to spend all her time thinking up ways of innocently seeing Jeremiah, and then endeavouring to suppress her giggles and restrain his hands. A favourite place was the walled garden. She would hang the washing out in the orchard and then slip quietly through the gate. Jeremiah would be waiting and they would steal a few precious moments together. Their delight in each other grew into a passion and they took more and more risks. Sometimes Kitty would creep into the stables or the tack room where Jeremiah cleaned the leathers. The smell of horses, linked as it was with their snatched kisses and hasty fumblings, she would forever associate with their illicit trysts. Kitty could not always conceal the excited blush to her cheeks and in her newly found love she embraced everyone she met with her joy, including John McCready.

Mrs. Welby watched events with troubled eyes and exchanged looks of concern with Jenny. She didn't miss much and didn't want to interfere but one day she felt compelled to offer a warning. 'I think you should take care.' she said, holding Kitty's arm in serious concern. 'You're playing with fire.' Kitty squirmed and snatched her arm away, irritated by the inference that she was doing wrong, but made no reply. She wasn't ready to think her situation through yet. One day she would. Soon.

Jeremiah brushed the black coats of Henry and Rupert until they shone and then forked clean straw down in the stalls. He turned around to find Jed leaning against the stable wall, watching him.

'Jed, you old rogue. Why do you always creep up so silently?' Jeremiah laughed . Whilst being totally different characters, the two young men got along well and enjoyed a mutual respect.

Jed smiled, pleased with himself that Jeremiah had not heard his approach. 'My job to creep around. Folks never know where I might be.'

'Move over, boy.' Jeremiah slapped Henry's rump and sat down in the manger near to Jed. 'So, what's up, then? No poachers to shoot at today?'

'None as I've seen. Plenty of other things to see though.' Jed eased himself down and selected a clean piece of straw to put between his teeth. He was wearing what he always wore – baggy brown trousers, rough jacket and slouch hat over his long black hair. A silence developed. Jeremiah was used to this. If there was something on Jed's mind, he'd get to it in his own time.

Eventually he said 'Pretty, ain't she.'

Jeremiah looked at his friend. 'I suppose you mean Kitty. Yes. Yes, she is.'

'McCready likes her. I seen him with her. Seen you too.' Jed took off his hat and scratched his head.

'You shouldn't spy on people. It's not right.'

'T'ain't spying if you happen to be where I happen to be. Seems to me she ought to make her mind up. You too.'

'Jed, I do believe you're jealous. I bet you like her too.'

'Maybe. But she wouldn't look twice at the likes of me.' Jed got up and knocked the straw off. 'Said my piece.' He nodded to Jeremiah and left the stables.

Jeremiah stayed sitting in the manger. He absently stroked the soft muzzle that came to explore his face as he sat mulling over the clipped words that passed for conversation with Jed. Perhaps he was right. Perhaps he should make his mind up – and quickly before McCready got any ideas.

Very soon the geldings needed to be re-shod. Jeremiah rode one and led the other down to the blacksmith's forge in Caunton. He could hear the clanking of the horseshoes being beaten into shape from the end of the street.

'Be with you afore long, Jemmy.' Walt Pinter called out as he bent down and picked up a hind hoof of farmer Todd's old cob. Resting the hoof on his leather apron, he proceeded to nail the shoe in place. The docile mare was so unconcerned that her head went down and she dozed peacefully in the sun. When he was satisfied with the shoe, Walt straightened up and wiped the sweat from his forehead. He led the mare around the corner and tethered her to a stake, where she could doze a little more before being collected.

Walt's bulging muscles threatened to burst through his shirt and the width around his girth was of such circumference as to make him almost as wide as he was high. He also had the widest smile and the warmest heart and he had liked Jeremiah from the moment he met him. He knew a good horseman when he saw one and this boy was the best. 'Jemmy, lad. I thought you'd about forgotten old Walt. So important you are now with the politicking an' all. I heard about the speech in the market place. And you, right in the middle of it all. Was it true about the fighting? Well, bless me!'

Jeremiah tethered the horses and followed Walt inside the forge. The heat was intense but Walt was not satisfied and handed Jeremiah a pair of bellows. 'Unless we want to be here all afternoon, Jemmy, we'd better put these to use.' More coals went on and soon the flames were licking up high and then settling down to a fierce heat. Their cheeks grew red and shiny. Walt began to remove the old shoes.

'Do you know much about love, Walt?' Jeremiah suddenly asked.

Walt looked up in surprise. 'Well, by Jove, Jem, what sort of a question is that to ask a man when he's going about his business? The file rasped back and forth over the shoeless hoof. The horse looked around inquisitively at the bent-over form of the blacksmith.

'It's just that – well, when you know and like a lot of girls, how do you know if the one girl you like the most is really the one that you love?'

Walt put down the hoof and looked at Jeremiah's earnest face. He threw his head back and laughed, exposing more gaps than teeth. 'I've been asked to give my opinion on a few things in my time, mostly horses you understand, but never about love, Jem. No. Never.' Relenting a little, he walked across and stood in front of Jeremiah, his massive arms folded across his chest. 'But love is a serious business, you can be sure. Especially at your age. Now, as I see it, there's liking, there's liking a lot and then there's loving. Is it that pretty lass working up at the Hall? Blue eyes and blond curls? Thought as much. Well now, my Missus ain't no picture but I know I love her. Do you want to know how I know that, Jem?' Jeremiah nodded. 'Because I would die for her. I would give my life for her. Simple. You ask yourself that question and when the answer comes back, you'll know. Now.' he said briskly, 'let's get on with the shoeing before we lose the heat again.'

Jeremiah rode the horses slowly back home. He asked himself the question – and the answer came back to him.

John McCready brought the invitation into the dining room on a silver tray. He offered it to Samuel Bristowe who opened it with the silver letter opener. He had pushed away his breakfast plate of kidneys and bacon and finished his second cup of coffee. His face brightened as he read and he looked up at his wife at the other end of the table.

'We have an invitation, my dear. From the Manor. Mr. & Mrs. Hole are asking if we would accompany them to a dinner at the town hall in Newark. This coming Saturday. We are to be conveyed in their carriage and stay the night at the Clinton Arms. Returning Sunday afternoon. What do you say, Sarah? Do you think you would be up to it?'

Sarah Bristowe watched her husband's face as he told her about the invitation and knew it meant a lot to him. Since coming here, he had been eager to be accepted by the local gentry as well as to take his share of the responsibility for the community. And now this politics thing. He seemed to be making a great many enemies with his Liberalism. To be seen with the Holes, major employers at the brewery in Newark, would certainly give his social standing a boost.

'Yes, of course, Samuel. I would like that very much.' She said brightly. 'The change and the company would do me the world of good.'

'Splendid, Sarah!' Samuel leapt up and kissed his wife's cheek. 'I'll send the reply straight away. You finish your breakfast, my dear.' He hurried off to his study to respond to the invitation.

Sarah looked down at her plate with the tiny portion of bacon on it and pushed it away. Her face was pinched and drawn. They seemed to have done so much entertaining

75

lately and it was all so exhausting. A social trip to Newark was the last thing she wanted to undertake but she was prepared to make the effort for her husband. He was working so hard to do the right thing, trying to make changes which in the short term would make his position difficult. She would not let him down.

McCready informed the servants of the arrangements for Saturday. Jeremiah would not be required, nor indeed would Mrs. Welby. Being overdue for a day off, Mrs.Welby saw the opportunity and asked if she could take the carrier's cart to Ollerton on the Saturday afternoon to see her sister. She would stay overnight and return on the Sunday afternoon in time to prepare the tea. Jenny Cocking would return to Kersall to see her mother. Everyone seemed happy with the arrangements.

The Saturday afternoon brought a flurry of preparations for the trip and the overnight stay. Mrs. Bristowe put on her prettiest dress and her brightest smile. Mr. & Mrs. Hole arrived in their splendid coach pulled by four matched greys and everyone set off for Newark in high spirits. Mrs. Welby prepared to walk down to the village and Kitty asked McCready if she could go with her and call and see her friend in Caunton. Anxious to please, he agreed. As they walked side by side, Mrs. Welby chatted about her sister and her family and how pleased she was to be seeing them again. 'I suppose I'll barely recognise some of the children – they'll have grown so.' she said excitedly. It crossed her mind to issue another warning to Kitty but as they turned the last bend she could see the cart already on its way up the hill. 'My word. Not a minute to spare.' she said, hurrying the last few yards. She waved gaily to Kitty from the cart as it continued on up the hill on its way to Ollerton. At least, she thought to herself, Kitty was going to see her friend so perhaps from now on she would stay away from that roguish Jeremiah.

Kitty took the road into Caunton right enough but as she turned a corner, there was Jeremiah waiting for her. He leapt out from behind a tree, caught her by the waist and swung her around. They both laughed until they were breathless. 'I thought he might not let you come.' he said at last.

'I told you. I can get whatever I want. I just have to say the right things.'

Jeremiah suddenly grew serious and his face changed to disapproval.

'You're not jealous are you?' Kitty asked. 'There's no need to be. He's a strange man, you know that. He just likes me, that's all.' She shrugged dismissively.

'You encourage him. I've seen you.'

'Well what's wrong with that. If being nice to him makes my life easier for once, why shouldn't I do it? I've been in service since I was thirteen and made to work like a slave. Now I get away with a few things. There's no harm in that, is there?' Kitty's face became petulant and she pulled her hands away from Jeremiah.

'You take too many liberties.'

Kitty sulked as they started to walk towards the beck Jeremiah still did not recover his humour. He was troubled by the situation. 'We need to be careful, you and I. He likes you more than you think. He could make life very difficult for us.' They reached the stream and walked along until they came to a section which was lined with old oaks and dense undergrowth. Jeremiah searched for a certain spot and then beckoned Kitty to push through a tiny gap. As they emerged through the bushes they found themselves in a secluded area. The shallow stream trickled through, bordered by soft earth and leaves. It tumbled lazily over a few stones and reflected the dappled light of the sky through the trees. Kitty's face lit up and she laughed delightedly. Jeremiah smiled. He knew she would be captivated by this secret place.

Their kisses were warm and sweet and, for once, unhurried. There was little chance they could be seen here but still Jeremiah did not recover his normal carefree manner. He seemed pensive and nervous.

'What is it? Have I done something wrong?' Kitty asked, her heart sinking. Jeremiah lifted his rough hand to gently stroke her cheek. He caressed her hair and followed the line of each curl with his fingers. He swallowed hard and still didn't speak. An age seemed to pass whilst Kitty listened to the trickle of the stream and smelled the damp earth. Her eyes began to well and a lump formed in her throat. He had come to mean so much to her and now he was growing distant. Perhaps he had found someone else. Just when she thought she ought to leave, Jeremiah, with no preamble, suddenly said 'Will you marry me?'

Kitty's blue eyes opened wide. For the moment, she was unable to speak.

'I really love you, Kitty. I love looking at you and being with you and I want to be with you all the time. Please say yes.' Jeremiah's solemn voice and earnest manner quite took her back but not for long. Relief flooded through her.

'Oh, yes. Yes, I'll marry you.' Kitty knew that she had fallen in love with Jeremiah and could only marvel in the fact that he loved her too. They kissed passionately and revelled in the closeness of their bodies. They were made for each other. Lost in the joy of knowing that they would spend their lives together, the warmth of their love washed over them and for those few precious moments, the world was theirs.

'Shall we tell everyone tomorrow – when they all come back?' Jeremiah was anxious to have their intended union made public. 'And you must change the way you speak to Mr. McCready. It won't do now, Kitty.'

They continued to make plans and kissed tenderly but their stolen time in the leafy haven ran out all too soon. They heard the church clock strike and reluctantly emerged from their secret place. From a nearby field Jed saw them and watched as they stole one last kiss. Kitty had to run most of the way back down the road to Beesthorpe but she felt so elated she could have run for miles. Jeremiah waited back a while. Just one more day, then everyone would know. Everyone. Including McCready.

Kitty stopped running at the gates to the Hall and tried to enter the kitchen not out of breath, but was greeted by McCready.

'I saw you running, Kitty. Is anything the matter?'

'No, no. I was just concerned about the time. Shall I prepare supper?'

'Mrs. Welby has left it all for us in the pantry. Shall Jeremiah be joining us?'

'I think so, yes. I'll lay the table.'

The clatter of the crockery on the wooden table seemed awfully loud as Kitty strained her ears for some sound of Jeremiah's arrival. She set the three places at the table quite far apart. In the centre she placed the pork pie Mrs. Welby had made, a dish of cold potatoes and a jar of pickled onions. She started as McCready suddenly appeared behind her and touched her elbow. 'You forgot the bread, Kitty.' He laid a squat loaf on a board with a large knife beside it.

The loud click of the heavy latch on the kitchen door signalled Jeremiah's arrival. 'Good evening Mr. McCready. Kitty.' he said stiffly.

'Good evening, Jeremiah.'

McCready picked up the knife and started a sawing action to penetrate the crusty loaf. Then he hacked a portion of the pork pie and handed the plate to Jeremiah. 'Kitty – the same for you?'

'Thank you Mr. McCready.' How she was going to swallow any food at all, Kitty had no idea. She must try to act normally. 'I hope Mrs. Welby is having a nice time with her sister. She was so looking forward to it. As we walked down the drive this afternoon she said to me how very much she was looking forward to seeing her sister. And her sister's children.' she blurted out rapidly. 'And Mrs. Bristowe. I hope she enjoys herself too.'

McCready smiled indulgently. 'And your friend, Kitty? How did you find your friend this afternoon?'

'Oh, well, thank you. Yes very well. Really quite well, I think. We had a very nice time. Thank you.' Flustered, she attacked the pork pie vigorously.

McCready turned to the silent Jeremiah. 'It must be strange for you to be here instead of the Ram stableyard.'

'Yes, Sir. Very strange. I seem to spend a lot of time there lately.'

'Indeed.'

Jeremiah, ill at ease, offered the jar of pickles around but no one wanted them. Kitty tried hard to chew the pork pie but it refused to reduce in her mouth. McCready ate slowly too. He seemed to be pondering on something. A strained silence settled. There was just the sound of knives and forks scraping on plates.

John McCready, lost in his own thoughts, noticed nothing. He totally failed to see the discomfort of the two young people, concentrating so fully, as he was, on his own thoughts – that is thoughts of Kitty and how best to declare his love. Her warmth towards him lately had given him great hope. She had bestowed upon him small kindnesses and much charm and he loved her for it. He had tried to make the conversation easier this evening but, of course, it hadn't worked. He always found it hard – but who knew how things would change for him if Kitty would agree to be his.

Silently, McCready cursed the fact that Jeremiah was not required for work that evening. If only he had been, then Kitty and himself would be alone together. He would have had plenty of time to put his thoughts and then his words together. He cast the young coachman a black look. He must find a means of sending him on his way and then speak to Kitty alone, without fear of interruption. He tried to rehearse the words in his head. It wasn't easy.

Kitty started to scrape and stack the plates. McCready didn't even notice the two patches of high colour that had developed on her cheeks. He sat deep in his own imaginary world, where everything worked out for the best and Kitty loved him. By the time he pushed his chair back from the table and reached for his tobacco to fill his pipe, he noticed that Jeremiah had disappeared. He looked around the kitchen in disbelief. His moment had come. At the sink, the object of his adoration stood pouring water from a jug into a bowl. She washed the dishes methodically, dried them and stacked them up. She started to take them back to the scullery. Back and forth she went. McCready silently drew on his pipe and watched, half dreading the moment when she would bid him goodnight and he would ask her to sit down because he had something to say to her.

How long it took him to realise that she had not returned but had slipped silently up the back stairs, he didn't know. Disappointment clouded his face. How could she leave without a word? It was not like her at all. He stayed in his chair in the silent kitchen, puffing clouds of smoke and pondering his dilemma. Should he go after her? That would be unseemly. Should he wait and speak to her in the morning? That would be too late for him. He felt very strongly that his future would be decided tonight. If there were to be any chance of happiness for him, he must act now.

Eventually, McCready put down his pipe and stood up. He crossed the kitchen and bolted the door. Then he walked slowly through to the hall to do his rounds and secure the house for the night. She mightn't yet be asleep. Perhaps there was still a chance he could talk to her. Fearful that the words would not come out properly and that he ran the risk of frightening her off, he slowly climbed the stairs.

Twilight was descending as McCready made his way up the grand staircase and along the main landing. The second staircase, leading up to the servants quarters in the attic, was narrow and dark. In the fading light he could make out a mouse scampering off down the corridor. His own room lay to the left, but Kitty's was down to the right. Resolute at last, his indecision finally banished, McCready stood in front of Kitty's attic bedroom door. His hand was raised to knock and call out her name, when he heard a sound from within. He realised it was Kitty's unmistakable giggle. Puzzled, he hesitated, his hand still raised. A further sound, a different voice, prompted him to bend down to peer through the keyhole.

He could distinguish little at first but slowly realised he could make out a boot – it was not Kitty's. Jeremiah's distinctive, knee-high, leather boots were on Kitty's bedroom floor. McCready's heart lurched as he heard their low, murmuring voices and squeaks from the bed. No! How could this be? How long had it been going on? The questions sprang unbidden to his tortured mind. He straightened up, his eyes full of hurt, and staggered away from the door.

He was in turmoil. Was he to be excluded forever from emotional fulfilment and physical pleasure? What could life hold for him now but bitterness and pain? How could she lead him on to think he had a chance, when all the time she had been won by a boy, a physical runt of no account? Bewilderment and mental questioning turned to pain and his eyes hardened. His chest felt like a block of stone and he stumbled down the stairs. Lurching across the kitchen, he yanked back the heavy bolt and burst through the door and out into the garden.

He gulped greedily at the evening air, like a drowning man. The rapidly diminishing light made no difference to McCready's vision, clouded as it was by the hate now surging through him like a furnace. As he staggered forward, he knocked an axe, carelessly left beside a pile of wood and, instantly siezing it, he raised it high over his head in an act of violent rage. With full force, he swung it at a log and split it open. The physical action and the searing sound gave him satisfaction, but far from diminishing, his rage was fuelled. The pent-up fury caused by his social inabilities exploded within him like a volcano, and reason and sanity were over-run by the fall-out. He raised his contorted face to the darkening sky and let forth a cry of pain. Retribution was the only thought as he charged back up the stairs to the top of the house. This time he would not be the victim. This time those who hurt him would suffer. Never again would he be passed over and cast aside to nurse his wounds alone and unloved.

The axe penetrated the door at the first blow. He felt that he was invincible as he swung it back and hurled it again and again, his super-human strength reducing the door to splinters in seconds. His huge frame blocked the doorway to the tiny room and he stood facing the perpetrators of the crime against him. Kitty's screams and Jeremiah's stricken face were lost on him. He did not allow them to occupy his consciousness. Dimly, he was aware of Kitty's naked breasts and beautiful, long hair, but now they represented loss and pain and failed to create a chink in the armour of his hatred. Murder was in

83

his heart and it must be sated. Driven by this desire alone, McCready advanced on the young couple and swung the axe.

Jeremiah instinctively rolled to one side and the blade struck the mattress alongside Kitty. Her eyes were filled with terror and she could not believe what was happening. McCready had gone mad! Screaming and nearly demented with fear, she pressed herself up to the wall, cowering under her own arms. Jeremiah's naked, pathetic little body was no match for McCready and his only advantage was his agility. He knew their lives depended on it and he used all his instincts to try to divert the madman, so that Kitty might slip past him to safety.

'Run, Kitty, run!' Jeremiah shouted.

Whether she heard or not, there was no response, but McCready, frustrated at swinging at and repeatedly missing his nimble quarry, decided to wreak his vengeance on the prostrate target. He turned to Kitty and swung the axe. Jeremiah leapt at him and with all his strength hurled himself at McCready's arm. The axe bit into the wall. Siezing the moment, Jeremiah reached forward to grab Kitty's arm to pull her to safety. McCready blocked his retreat in an instant and in the confined space, Jeremiah had no escape. For a second they looked into each other's eyes and each knew the outcome. Jeremiah prepared to meet his maker and McCready the road to hell.

The blade sliced and smashed into Jeremiah's fragile body with a sickening sound. From neck to chest his flesh and bones were exposed like a rabbit under the butcher's knife. The bed, the floor, the walls and Kitty were drenched in the hot sticky lifeblood of the handsome young man gurgling his last breath on the bed beside her. Sobbing yet immobile with shock, Kitty lay curled up by the wall, unable to protect herself.

McCready stood in the centre of the room, breathing heavily. The bloodied axe in his hand was still raised but he did not move. Gradually, the fearsome expression left his features and the hate-filled eyes slowly narrowed as he looked at the grisly scene before him and saw the consequences of his insane actions. He lowered the axe and let it fall to the floor. Kitty's naked back was so close to him. He reached out a hand to touch the soft, warm flesh. How many times had he dreamed of this moment? God knows, it had occupied his thoughts night and day for weeks. His breath came in husky rasps as desire surged through him. She continued to sob and remained turned away, trying desperately to shut everything out. McCready's trembling hand slowly caressed the white back. She was his now. He had the power of the moment. He could do with her as he wished. But as his hand travelled down her back, the blood in his veins turn to ice. Cold reality washed over him and he turned away from the naked girl. After some moments, he bent down to scoop up the broken body of the young boy. Blood still ran from him, leaving a macabre trail as McCready carried him down the stairs. With each step, cruel sanity returned. 'What, in God's name, have I done?' he whispered. 'Dear Lord, how has this happened? I searched for happiness and it has taken me to Hell.' He bowed his head and stared in disbelief as the evidence of his madness lay, lifeless, in his arms.

McCready stood outside the kitchen door and bellowed to the sky. 'No. No.' He shook his head from side to side, vainly trying to deny the wretched nausea which engulfed him. The garden, devoid of all colour in the fading light, was like his life. Night had come and morning would never break.

'He robbed me.' McCready sobbed, still cradling Jeremiah in his arms. 'He robbed me of all happiness. All life. He could have had any girl he wanted. Why did it have to be Kitty? Why my love? He couldn't have needed her the way I did.' Tears spilled from his eyes as he ranted on to the empty sky above him. Anguished sobs wracked his body as the night descended and enclosed him like a shroud. Eventually, McCready staggered inside the wash-house and laid Jeremiah down.

The dawn of the new day found two bodies at Beesthorpe Hall. Jeremiah, with his hacked chest and lolling head, lay obscenely over the copper. Above him, the rope creaked as McCready's corpse swung gently back and forth, his earthly trials now over, but his soul damned to hell for eternity.

CHAPTER TEN
The Aftermath

JED patrolled back through the woods, his gun resting in the crook of his arm. He picked up the sound of voices in the garden of the Hall and could recognise, even from a distance, that the tone was amiss for a Sunday afternoon. All his instincts came to the fore. Something was wrong. Without snapping a twig or making one sound, he cautiously worked his way through the trees and down to the very edge of the back garden. From the safety of his camouflage he peered through the leaves and scrutinized the scene before him. His black eyebrows came together in a heavy frown.

The farmers from the two neighbouring farms were standing awkwardly outside the wash-house. They looked uncomfortable with their caps in their hands, and even their low mutterings ceased as Samuel Bristowe emerged through the wash-house door. His face was stricken. He covered his mouth with his hand and turned away from the men, breathing deeply. One of the farmers' wives appeared around the side of the house, scuttling past with her head turned aside, and hastily let herself in through the kitchen door.

Breaking his cover, Jed emerged onto the lawn and slowly approached the group. They saw him coming but seemed unwilling or unable to acknowledge him by either word or action. He walked right up and looked at them questioningly. Reluctantly, they met his gaze.

'There's been a bad going-on. Two dead men in there.'

Jed stood in silent astonishment.

Samuel Bristowe remained apart from the others. He could not look at Jed and was still struggling to control himself. 'A tragedy.' was all he managed to whisper.

Full of dread, the young gamekeeper approached the door to the wash-house. Before he had even crossed the threshold he could see the legs dangling and he stood transfixed, mesmerised by the tiny swaying movement, his ears catching the intermittent creak of the rope. Still unable to fathom the identity, he entered and looked up. Dear God. McCready! In staring so incredulously at the twisted face of the corpse above his head, Jed was aware of nothing else. When finally he lowered his eyes it was with horror that he saw his friend, Jeremiah. The naked body was marble white and his neck and chest gashed bloody and ragged. His face, framed with his brown hair, looked unreal. Flies began to buzz and settle on the congealed blood.

Jed stumbled out of the door. He pulled the hat from his head and stared uncomprehendingly at the ground. 'Where's Kitty?' he whispered. No-one spoke.

At the sound of horses, they all looked up. From the village the vicar had driven himself down in a buggy, closely followed by the Parish Constable, on horseback.

'I have sent to Southwell for the High Constable. And I am bidden by Mrs. Hole to say she is expecting Mrs. Bristowe to be her guest as soon as ever is convenient.'

Samuel Bristowe nodded to the constable. It was ironic that no sooner had the Hole's coach dropped them off and begun back down the drive that Mrs. Welby had, rather hysterically, informed him that something was seriously wrong. Kitty was incoherent, bloodstained and in a state of shock and McCready was nowhere to be seen. They had followed the trail and made the discovery. One of the farmers' boys had been dispatched to Caunton.

Samuel Bristowe began to think in terms of priority now and his wife's health was at the forefront of his mind. He must get her away from the house. Her fragile state of mind would not cope with this hideous event

88

taking place in her very own home. He summoned Jed to him and put a hand on his shoulder. 'I know this is hard for you – as it is for us all. Jed, I need you to drive the coach to take Mrs. Bristowe down to Caunton. You're good with horses. I know you are. Will you do that for me?'

'Jed nodded slowly. 'Yes, I can do that.'

'Bring the coach to the front of the house as soon as you can.'

Jed set off for the stables. Jeremiah had left the tack hung neatly from pegs on the wall. The dullness in the pit of his stomach intensified as he forced his mind to work out how exactly to accomplish the task of preparing the horses for the traces. He wished he had taken more heed when he had spent time with Jeremiah. Considering the unfamiliar nature of the job, and except for one or two buckles needing to be worked out, he finally succeeded. The horses obeyed him but were skittish with their inexperienced driver. It was only a couple of miles but Jed was relieved when the journey was made and Mrs. Bristowe stepped down from the coach to be welcolmed into the arms of Mrs. Hole.

'Thank you, Jed.' She turned her pale face back to him and smiled before making her shaky way to the door.

'Ma'am.' said Jed, nodding acknowledgement.

Although lowly born and a rough, country youth with no education, Jed was aware of how things should be and he felt conscious of his appearance. His rough coat and dirty leggings belonged to the woods, not on Mr. Bristowe's shiny black coach with the brass lamps and thoroughbred horses. He was uneasy in his new role and was glad when he had successfully negotiated the journey home.

McCready, with the help of the farmers, had been cut down and laid on the other side of the room from Jeremiah. Both bodies were covered in sacking. The vicar, having issued his pastoral care, returned to Caunton to be in time for the evening service.

'The constable needs to make a report, Jed.' said Samuel Bristowe. 'We shall all of us have to say what we know. Go into the kitchen to Mrs. Welby and wait there.'

Jed opened the kitchen door but stood still, uncertain as to whether he should enter. Daylight had all but gone but no lamp lit the room. From a distant corner, Mrs. Welby's voice carried to him. 'Come in. Fill that kettle and boil water for tea.' He could hear the sound of water being squeezed from a cloth. 'There we are, dear. Nearly all gone. It's only Jed, come to help.'

Jed realised that it was Kitty sitting in a chair, wrapped in a blanket and being cleaned up by Mrs. Welby. Her eyes stared out unseeingly and her hair, damp from the wet cloth, lay flat to her head. Mrs. Welby began to brush it methodically. Jed felt extremely ill at ease.

After some time, hard ridden horses pulled up outside the front door. A succession of lamps passed the kitchen window, on their way to the wash-house. Voices could be heard. Eventually the kitchen door opened and two strangers, the High Constable and his aide, came in with Samuel Bristowe. Their black cloaks and sombre faces filled the room. They started with the questions. Samuel Bristowe answered and so did Mrs. Welby. The constable came to Kitty. She looked at him through lifeless eyes. When at last, she spoke it was with a flat, matter-of-fact tone, made doubly shocking by the simple description of the nightmare through which she had lived.

The man said 'Thank you, Miss.' and Mrs. Welby led her from the room.

'Did you have no insight into the underlying tensions in your household, Mr. Bristowe?'

'No. I am ashamed to say, I did not. None at all. I have, of course, been very busy lately – the election you see.'

The inquisitor turned to Jed. 'And you. Were you aware of rivalry? Of unspoken affections?'

This was a tricky one for Jed. With his habit of fading into the background, he had seen a great deal. He had witnessed McCready helping Kitty in the orchard. He'd seen the way she looked at him with her warm smiles and her head cocked prettily to one side. The encouragement was obvious. Then it was Kitty and Jeremiah creeping about in the walled garden and the stables. He'd even witnessed their passionate kisses with their hands all over each other, when they had no idea they were being observed. It had been hard not to have a pang of envy of Jeremiah. He had been so confident and lively and so loved by everyone he met. Jed was sure that at least two of his sisters were in love with him. But lately he only had eyes for Kitty.

Jed shifted uneasily and did not look up. 'Well, Sir. No. I mean, I seen them – Kitty with Mr. McCready but workin' o'course. But no affections. No, Sir.'

Mrs. Welby re-entered the room and the same question was asked of her.

'Well, I never. What a thing to suggest! There was no improper behaviour in my kitchen – nor underlying tensions, as you put it.'

'May we now see the scene of the crime, Mr. Bristowe?'

Armed with lamps and candles, the men re-traced McCready's steps of the previous night. The sight of the smashed door brought unbidden gasps of awe. Splintered wood lay all about. Raw, exposed timber with jagged points told of the violence and within the room, the bloodstained walls and hacked mattress added a grim eloquence. The axe lay, discarded.

At last the constable was satisfied that the story related was the truth. 'My only concern is the girl. Did she inflame the hearts of these men wilfully? If so, then she is responsible for the crime and should be punished accordingly.'

Samuel Bristowe spoke up. 'I assure you, Sir, that although the girl has not been in my employ for very long, she came with good references and has shown nothing but diligence and correctness of manner in all things. I have no hesitation in speaking for her.'

'I shall, of course, make my report to the magistrate. If it is accepted, then so be it. I'll get word to you about the burial tomorrow.'

As the men re-mounted their horses, Samuel Bristowe came out of the house with two glasses of brandy 'To warm you before your return journey, gentlemen.' Gratefully, they tipped the fiery liquid to the back of their throats before galloping off into the night.

Early the next morning, Jed reported to the house, as requested. From the village, Billy White, the carpenter, arrived with one coffin loaded up on his cart. He and Jed carried it round to the wash-house and laid Jeremiah's body to rest inside it. They nailed the lid down.

Billy scratched his beard and looked down at McCready's body. 'Suicide burial then.'

'Seems so.' said Jed.

Samuel Bristowe walked towards them. His face was strained. 'Arrangements have been made for the burial of Jeremiah in the churchyard this afternoon.' he said.

Jed and Billy drove the creaking cart bearing the coffin down to Caunton in the full heat of the summer afternoon. Samuel Bristowe rode behind. At three o'clock they pulled up outside the churchyard. The funeral bell tolled and a group of villagers assembled to bid farewell to the young man they had come to love. The sadler, the tailor, the cobbler and the shopkeeper – all knew how much they were going to miss the carefree young man. Walt Pinter looked uncomfortable, squeezed into his best

Sunday coat, but the tears in his eyes were for the young man who had asked him about love. He recalled his reply. Poor Jem really had loved her after all. And he had died for her.

Half a dozen girls stood together, crying quietly. There were no relatives. Kitty did not attend.

As they walked away Samuel Bristowe came up to Jed. 'We are awaiting confirmation, but I think it will be tonight. Be at the house by nine o'clock.'

Jed nodded.

The appointed hour came but no word had been received. The light was fading. 'We only got 'til midnight. Must be finished by then.' Billy said. 'If we don't start out soon it'll be too late.' He paused. 'Not leaving the body for all to see, then?'

'No. Mr. Bristowe thinks it too disrespectful. So do I.' Jed kept his eyes focused on the long drive. He wanted it over tonight. At last a horseman appeared, galloping hard. The constable dismounted and Samuel Bristowe, who had also been watching anxiously from the house, came to the door.

'I have ridden straight from Southwell.' the constable reported breathlessly. 'We have permission for the burial tonight. Samuel Bristowe nodded to Jed and Billy and they immediately turned to load the body on the cart.

'Do you have everything? You know exactly what is required?' the constable asked.

'We know.' said Jed.

The cart rattled off down the drive. The evening air was warm and still and the light was fading fast. Bats darted by, feeding on hovering insects. After the heat of the day, Jed could quite distinctly detect the sickly smell of the corpse begining to decompose. The sacking covering McCready's body did not quite cover his feet and as the cart jolted on, more of him became exposed. In accordance with the rules, his body had been stripped, but even greater indignity awaited him that night.

They continued on down the Newark road towards the Caunton crossroads with the constable following behind on horseback. No-one was about, the road was deserted. At the crossroads they stopped under the boughs of an ancient wych elm. Jed lit the oil lamp, held it aloft in the darkness and searched for a suitable place. Just beyond where the gnarled branches dipped low to the ground, he and Billy started to dig. The soft earth gave willingly under their spades but it had to be a large grave and they must have the task over and done with by midnight. From a distant homestead, a dog set up a solitary barking. They straightened and turned their heads as the church clock struck eleven.

'How are you doing there?' the constable held the lamp to inspect the progress.

'Not long now.' Sweat trickled down Jed's face. He wasn't a particularly religious man but he didn't agree with this. It seemed a high price to pay for a moment of madness. McCready had not been a wicked man. He had been good to him, had shown him respect and Jed didn't like to think of him denied his eternal salvation. The grave was at last completed and Billy and Jed removed the sacking and laid the naked corpse into the ground. The constable watched.

'Now the stake.' he ordered.

Jed walked back to the cart and took out a wooden stake and a hammer. He didn't want to do this. A half moon had risen and shed a pale light into the grave. The white body was clearly visible against the dark earth but still Billy held the lamp high. Jed had his back to the constable. He placed the stake over McCready's heart and raised the hammer. He hesitated.

'Get on with it.' the constable urged.

With all his might, Jed brought the hammer down. The stake bore down into the soft earth at the side of McCready's body. Billy looked up into Jed's eyes. Jed stared back. 'It's done.' he said. Hastily, he scattered quick lime over the body and the two men started to fill in the grave.

'No prayers.' the constable ordered. The two men stood silently, looking down at the fresh earth.

'Poor bugger.' Billy said before replacing his cap.

The deed was done with ten minutes to spare. The constable bid them goodnight and rode home. Billy took Jed some way in the cart before turning into the lane to his own home. The clock struck midnight. 'Did you do right, Jed?' he asked. 'The stake in the heart is meant to stop the ghost from walking. I wouldn't like to think we done wrong.'

'It wasn't wrong. No need to behave that way to a decent man, even if he was a murderer. Now he's dead. Should be an end of the matter.' Jed climbed down from the cart and looked back up at Billy. ' Not a word. Not a word to anyone.' Jed turned and continued back to Beesthorpe on foot. He felt a small pride that he had beaten the authorities. He'd done what he thought was right, for once.

McCready's name was never mentioned again.

Samuel Bristowe rode on horseback to visit his wife at The Manor. As Jed walked down through the parkland, he cantered up behind him. 'Another job for you, Jed. It's a lot to ask I know, but I think you can do it. I'd like you to drive the coach over to Derbyshire to take Mrs. Bristowe back to stay with my family for a while. Billy will be able to go with you to help. You can drive there in one day but you'll have to make good time. I'll look out a decent jacket and breeches for you to wear.'

Derbyshire! Jed was astounded. He'd only been to Newark once in his life. Half of him was proud that his employer trusted him both with his wife and his coach and horses, but half of him was scared. Would he find it? Would he be hopelessly lost?

Samuel Bristowe knew what Jed was thinking. 'Don't worry. I'll tell you very clearly how to get there and which Inns to call at for directions.'

Preparations were made. It helped Jed to take his mind off the loss of his friend and early the following morning they set out. It had been decided that Jenny Cocking, as her lady's maid, would accompany Mrs. Bristowe. Billy sat up next to Jed.

Beyond Southwell Jed said. 'You been along here before, Billy?

'I been as far as the Lowdham cotton mill, delivering wood once.' Billy shook his head as though trying to wipe out the memory. 'T'aint right. Apprentices they call 'em but they're just children working every hour of the day. Near starved, they looked, with their pallid, sickly faces and half suffocated by the foul air.' The cotton mill came into view and both men stared across at it. 'Them water wheels are mighty dangerous to be near. I seen a terrible accident to a child there. Terrible.' After a while, Billy managed to shake off the piteous memories of the apprentices and good-naturedly slapped Jed's shoulder. 'You and I are seeing the world today, boy. For what it's worth.' he chuckled.

They made their way to Nottingham and then out on the Sawley turnpike. The state of the roads varied and there always seemed to be a section or two being mended with crushed stones but Jed duly handed over the sum of two shillings at each toll house. Sometimes there was a problem when on-coming vehicles wanted to pass and the road was too narrow but generally they made good progress. Jed felt stiff in his formal jacket and after their brief rest stop at The Rose and Crown in Nottingham, he was anxious to get on.

The sights and sounds of such a large town were alarming to him. So many smart carriages and fine houses – and then, as far as the eye could see, streets and streets of squashed up houses with barely a lane between them, stretching off into the distance. Tall chimneys on grim factories belched out black smoke high into the sky. Jed could only feel pity for the poor people who worked in them, amongst the noise and the dangerous machinery, rarely enjoying the fresh air and sunshine. He thought of the children Billy had told him about. The world beyond Caunton held little attraction for him. He concentrated on the horses and making sure he was on the right road. Eventually, as night fell, having followed the instructions carefully, they arrived at their destination. Twyford was a small village on the banks of the Trent. Jed thought it flat and dismal but they found the Manor House easily enough. With their arrival, the door opened and light spilled out. Jenny Cocking went forward.

'If you please, Sir' she said to the butler 'Mrs. Sarah Bristowe.'

A booming voice behind him burst out of the hallway. 'Sarah, my dear. What has happened?' The old gentleman to whom the voice belonged opened the carriage door and helped Mrs. Bristowe down. Overcome by tiredness and emotion, she was unable to speak and fell into the arms of her husband's Uncle William. He was completely at a loss but led her into the house and the care of his wife. Jed climbed down from the coach. 'Sir. I have a letter, Sir. From Mr. Samuel Bristowe.' He reached into his coat pocket and handed over the creased paper.

Trunks were unloaded and orders and instructions issued. After Jed and Billy had found their way around to the stables and unharnessed the horses Uncle William came to them. 'I now understand the circumstances of

Mrs. Bristowe's arrival and greatly saddened I am, as will be everyone here – for John McCready was well known to us.' Jed nodded. 'Samuel speaks well of you and your help in conveying Sarah here. Now, make yourselves comfortable and rest. Ah, here is your supper.'

The stew and dumplings washed down with beer restored them considerably. Billy slept on the makeshift bed in the tackroom and Jed made himself at home in the hay next to the horses.

The next morning they departed for the return journey. There was plenty of time for talk and reflection but as they passed the wych elm at the Caunton crossroads they fell silent.

Election day was now nearing and Samuel Bristowe decided to go into Newark and to stay there, at the Ram Inn, until it was over. Jed drove him in and then returned home with the coach. He'd had all the excitement he needed and was grateful to get back to his woods and rabbits.

The scandal of Beesthorpe Hall, even though at below stairs level, did not help Samuel Bristowe's election campaign. When the opposition heard of it, the stories were twisted to become even more lurid. It was the talk of the whole county. Try as he might to return to the real issues of the day, someone would always bring up the murder. The power and passion of his speeches continued but somehow he felt he had lost conviction and his heart went out of the battle for reform. He knew he had great support – but would those who cheered him have the courage to act and actually make their vote for him?

In the end, the voting was close, but Samuel Bristowe was not returned as Member of Parliament for Newark. Many who wore the blue liberal colours to the polling station, voted for the reds – the conservatives. The Duke of Newcastle had won again. Samuel Bristowe returned to Beesthorpe to inform his servants that he was closing the house and returning to Twyford to join his wife. 'I have no knowledge of the length of time I shall be away' he said 'but when I do return, I expect the unfortunate events of the last weeks to be cast behind us. I forbid that it be spoken of again. Your jobs depend upon it.' Finally he added 'The door to the attic room has been replaced. It has been locked and will remain that way for always.'

No-one had seen Kitty since that night. Mrs. Welby ran the house as well as she could. Jed called on her every day to see if she needed anything. Very soon, an air of neglect prevailed. At Beesthorpe, life would never be the same again.

CHAPTER ELEVEN
Repercussions

THREE long months had passed since the night of the murder and life had not returned to normal at Beesthorpe Hall. It never would for those who had witnessed the scene, especially Kitty. The Bristowes had reluctantly returned to the house.

Samuel Bristowe stood by the window in the large drawing room, gazing down at the cows grazing peacefully in Lockabeck meadow. The scene was familiar and soothing, and for the moment he tried to put the events of the past few months out of his mind. He had taken his defeat badly. He felt he had let so many people down. People who had been counting on him to make changes. He could have had an influence and helped to improve the lives of so many. But those for whom he had been most responsible – his servants, he felt he had also failed. His wife's health had taken a considerable turn for the worse and this was now his main concern. Action had to be taken to clear the house of all connections with the hideous drama. His agitation returned as he heard the knock and the soft footfall on the polished oak floor. He turned and there stood Kitty.

The intervening weeks since he had last seen her had been difficult for them all. Although he knew Kitty had been severely traumatised, like everyone else, at the back of his mind was the feeling that she had caused it. To lead a man on was a wicked thing. When questioned, Mrs. Welby had been defensive of her but it was only because of his own testament to her character that she had been spared incarceration in the House of Correction. Samuel felt he had done his best for her but since the event her welfare had barely been in his thoughts, so he was totally

100

unprepared for the dramatic change in her appearance. Her pretty round cheeks were gaunt and hollow. She was frail and thin and her eyes were lifeless. No longer mischievous or playful, the light had gone out of them.

'Kitty, this is very hard for me to say, but I must. Mrs. Bristowe, as you know, is in a delicate condition and the doctor has advised she must not be distressed in any way. I had hoped that our prolonged absence from the house would have helped her to put the tragic incident out of her mind, but I'm afraid it has not. Your presence here can only increase her discomfort. I must ask you to find another position.' He paused but Kitty showed no response so he continued, 'I appreciate it may not be easy, but I should like you to go into Newark tomorrow to look for employment. Under the circumstances, of course, I cannot send you with a letter of recommendation. I will allow, however, that should you be unsuccessful, you may return and we will discuss the matter further, but I strictly forbid you to be observed by Mrs. Bristowe.'

'Thank you, Sir.' Kitty turned and left as softly as she had entered. She had expected it. Mrs. Welby had hinted as much. It didn't matter – nothing mattered.

It was a sultry August day and the two heavy horses pulling the carrier's cart from Ollerton to Newark needed constant encouragement to keep a steady pace. Kitty had walked into Caunton to wait for the cart and now she sat perched on a tiny portion of wooden seat. At her feet, two white chickens, tied together by their legs, looked up at her with their red beady eyes. She stared back at them. 'I am as helpless as you are. My life is no different.' she thought. 'Others will decide your fate, just as they will mine.'

Being market day, the road to Newark was busy. Men, women and children walked along carrying heavy bundles, and carts and wagons of all shapes and sizes creaked towards the town to trade. Sheep and cattle were driven along, sometimes one or two at a time, sometimes in small herds. The drovers with their sticks and the shepherds with their crooks, all wore their heavy country smocks and called encouragement to the animals. 'Get on there. On you go, girl.'

Everyone was heading into Newark so as the toll was paid at the entrance to the town, a queue formed on the bridge over the river. The cart in front was carrying a dead cow and flies buzzed around it as the heat of the day rose steadily.

Straight ahead was the cattle market. Pens of Shorthorn bullocks, fattened up for slaughter, and old drape cows, dried out and infertile, patiently awaited their fate. Newly shorn Border Leicesters and Lincolnshire longhorns bleated out their confusion. Farmers and dealers strolled between the pens, running their experienced hands over backs and rumps before settling down to hard bargaining. Kitty watched it all.

The road ahead was cluttered with carts piled high with wool but eventually everyone disembarked and dispersed to attend to their business. Kitty crossed the town and turned into the buttermarket. The coolness of the building, situated as it was underneath the Town Hall, was pleasant to the skin but full to bursting with traders making a great noise. The sound reverberated around the enclosed space, echoing off the stone columns. Kitty emerged into the airless market place and stood amongst the stalls piled high with vegetables, baskets, smocks and ironmongery. She stood quietly among the boisterous crowd because all she could see was Jeremiah's face – smiling and excited and holding up the ribbons against her hair. Slowly, her young lover's face receded and the reality of the day's mission returned. She had to find employment.

Over at the Wing Tavern, Mary scrutinized her friend. 'You look terrible, Kitty. So thin.'

'I'm alright really. But I need a job, Mary. Do they need anyone here? You know I'm a good worker.'

'You can't work here! The whole town knows what happened and you caused it. The stories we've been hearing, Kitty. Makes your flesh creep. Did you really sleep with both of them together? Is it true he hacked his heart out?'

'No, no. You don't understand.' Kitty protested.

'Well, I don't know what's to understand, I'm sure, but they won't want the likes of you here anyway.'

Kitty felt crushed by this cruel reception. Mary was her friend. How could she say such things? Hurt and bemused, she made her way over to the Queen's Head. The smell of beer and unwashed bodies rose up to meet her as she pushed open the door. Full of farmers out for market day, some smoked pipes and some ate hearty meals but they all drank from pint tankards and smelled of the farmyard. A serving girl pointed out the landlord to her.

'A job is it? Well now. Pretty you may be but you don't look as though you can work too hard. Where are you from then? Caunton you say. Some nasty goings on that way. Beesthorpe Hall? Why that was the very place! Are you the one who – yes, you look the sort. Well, on your way, my girl.' The story was almost the same at every coaching inn and tavern in Newark. Even the dye works and the brewing houses would not consider her. 'We don't want your sort here, causing trouble between decent men.'

The heat of the day grew more and more oppressive. People and horses sweated and the stench from the offal heap by the slaughterhouse yard, mingled with the sickly smell of the maltings, pervaded the whole town. Kitty felt weak and barely able to drag herself through the streets.

She sat down by the bear baiting post in the market place and fanned herself with her hat, oblivious to all the activity going on about her. It seemed so long ago that she had stood here among the crowd and felt such excitement. Now, she was isolated, lonely and rejected. And it was all her own fault. That was possibly the worst feeling of all – guilt. She could see it all so clearly. Why couldn't she before? Wrapped up in her own emotions, she had ruthlessly exploited McCready's to serve her own purpose. And Jeremiah had paid the price for her callousness with his life. It was degrading to realise what people were saying about her but in her heart she knew she deserved it. After the Constable's enquiry had been completed she had been largely left alone. Mr. Bristowe had spoken up for her and nothing further had been said until now.

By the time the carrier's cart set off for the return journey, the fetid humidity of the air was suffocating. From Beastmarket Hill Kitty glanced across at the unsavoury dregs of mankind at the castle shacks and shuddered. 'Will that be me one day? Begging, ragged, dirty and sick. Will I be offering myself to men for money – just to stay alive?'

The horses plodded their weary way and the sky grew close and threatening. As she climbed down from the cart at Caunton, the summer storm broke abruptly. Heavy drops of rain fell hard, crashing like lead shot on the trees and splashing back up as they hit the ground. Kitty didn't hurry. There was no point. Perhaps the rain would wash away her sins and she would be purified in the eyes of the Lord. Sheet lightning covered the whole valley in an ethereal light and thunder clapped directly over her head. It made her feel that she was solely responsible for the anger of the elements.

By the time Kitty reached the Hall she was drenched through. Her skirt clung to her legs and her hair hung like rats tails. She stood dripping on the flagstone floor of the kitchen and was unable to move. Mrs. Welby abandoned her pastry making and came across to her. It wasn't just the rain, there was an element of utter dejection about her – as though for the first time she was understanding the hopelessness of her situation. As Mrs. Welby reached out her hand to touch her, Kitty turned her head and tears spilled out to mingle with the raindrops on her cheeks.

'It's alright, dear.' Mrs. Welby spoke softly, as to a child. She could imagine the reception she would have had, looking for work. It hurt to see the young girl have to learn such a bitter lesson. Just when she thought the world was hers. She steered Kitty to a chair and held her hand whilst mopping at her wet face with her apron.

The warmth of the human touch and Mrs. Welby's gentleness brought a little life to the bedraggled girl. Kitty knew that the events of the day had jolted her out of the shock which had numbed her emotions for the last three months. Now, as if the storm was her awakening, she knew her precarious position. A violent shiver passed right through her.

Mrs. Welby fussed over her. 'Let's get these wet clothes off before you catch cold.' Kitty made no reply. 'No luck then.' she said softly. It wasn't a question.

Kitty looked her directly in the eye for the first time and said 'No. No-one will have me now.'

Kitty stood once more before Samuel Bristowe in the drawing room. Whilst she stood timidly by the door, he paced up and down by the windows. 'I believe I have made the position clear to you, Kitty. It is quite out of the question for you to remain here. Now, I appreciate the difficulty in finding a position. The scandal is still much in people's thoughts and, of course, you do carry a portion of blame. Some even suggest it to be a large portion. Do I understand correctly that you have no relatives to whom you could turn? None at all?'

Kitty shook her head, 'No Sir. None whatever.'

'Well now. Then there is only one option open to you. The workhouse at Southwell.

Kitty's head snapped up and her eyes searched her employer's face, looking for a sign – a different suggestion, some other way out for her. The workhouse? The word brought fear and dread. When faced with poverty it was only to be considered as an alternative to starvation – for those too sick or stupid to be gainfully employed and who would otherwise be in the gutter, an offence to society. Surely that could not be her? She knew it to be a life of toil without reward, of hardship without comfort and misery without hope. The reputation of the workhouse was so harsh that friends and relatives rallied to support each other in difficult times in order to keep that evil at bay. Anything but the workhouse.

Kitty had been in service since the age of thirteen, when Aunt Esther had died. She had no other relatives alive and no friends who would be prepared to help her now. All these thoughts crowded in on her as she struggled to grasp the enormity of this cruel decision.

'I think, under the circumstances, it would be for the best.' Samuel Bristowe continued, 'so I have a letter here for you to take with you. I know the Reverend Becher you see. And the Overseer of the Poor in Southwell is, I think, a fair man. So that is settled. You will make your way there tomorrow.' He turned to stare out of the window. No matter how hard it was on the girl, he had to think of his wife. There was nothing else to be done. If all else failed, the next step would be to rent out the house and move away – London perhaps. He could set up in a law firm and Sarah could enjoy good society. It could be the best solution for everyone. He turned around.

'Good luck to you, Kitty.' She was already through the door and did not hear his last words.

The next morning Kitty dressed herself in a daze. She could not believe what was happening. This unthinkable step to the workhouse was the ultimate degradation. Mrs. Welby tried her best to be positive. 'It's a new building, so I hear – the best in the country, so they say. It might not be as bad as people think. Well, at least it's somewhere to lay your head. Be alright, you'll see.' With a parting hug she wished Kitty luck and watched as the forlorn figure grew smaller and smaller in the distance. She shook her head and thought to herself 'Poor girl. She'll be sure to need every bit of luck she can get.'

Kitty trudged down the road, her feet heavy and her stomach churning. Unobserved, Jed watched her progress from the cover of the reeds down by the lake. She was hot and her coat and few belongings were awkward to carry. It was a beautiful day with a clear blue sky. She hesitated as she passed the road leading down into Caunton and then found that she had reached the churchyard. Hesitantly, she approached the new grave where the grass had not yet grown over. A simple wooden cross had been erected and someone had laid a bunch of bluebells beneath it. She wished she had thought to pick some flowers herself.

Kitty dropped to her knees and dug her hands deep into the soil. She held them up and the soft earth ran through her fingers. 'I'm so sorry, Jem. It was all my fault. I know that. Please forgive me.' She turned when she heard a cough behind her and there stood the blacksmith. He wiped his blackened hands self consciously on his leather apron. 'I saw you from across the way, Miss.' he indicated the forge on the other side of the road. 'I thought you might like to know that the villagers are going to buy a headstone – with his name and everything. Thought a lot of him, we did. A good lad.' Kitty did not answer but she attempted a smile and nodded slowly. Embarrassed, Walt turned away but then added 'He did love you, Miss.'

'I know.' she whispered.

The sunshine had dried everything and now the farmers were anxious to continue with the corn-cutting. Gangs of men were scything, working rythmically alongside each other, and the women bringing their dinner to the fields called out cheerfully. Carts overtook her and the occupants bid her good-day. The countryside colours were clean and fresh and everyone was happy – but then, they weren't going to the workhouse.

Kitty had never seen it, of course, let alone been inside, but the stories were chilling and the life, she knew, would be grim. All the more poignant that this should be a beautiful day, when the future looked so ugly. She sat down at the side of the track to rest and lay back in the lush grass, enjoying the sun warming her face, the insects humming around her and the heady scents of the wild flowers. It was like a parting gift – a sweet moment to carry with her.

Kitty forced herself on down the road. The twin towers of the Southwell Minster came into view but before the outskirts of the town she turned into a lane and there, on a hillside, stood the workhouse. It was enormous, high and imposing with small barrack-like windows and very few chimneys. It looked austere and regimented and, even on this beautiful day, cold and forbidding. Kitty stood before it and looked up at her prison windows. They seemed to mock her, 'Well, for all your pretty charms, it's here you've ended up.'

A door opened and a thick set woman with heavy jowls challenged her.

'Well? Are you for the workhouse?'

Kitty nodded, mutely. The woman simply jerked her head to one side and snapped 'Side door.'

Kitty walked across and stood there, overwhelmed with self-pity. Reluctant to take the final step she waited for a long time. Eventually, she mustered her courage and pushed on the heavy door to enter the workhouse – her spirit crushed, mentally scarred and pregnant.

CHAPTER TWELVE
The Workhouse

'WAIT here, I'll fetch the Master.' The woman disappeared, leaving Kitty looking at the bare walls of the small receiving room. There was no chair and she was struck by how cool it was inside, given the warm outdoor temperature. The Master arrived clasping a ledger tightly to his chest as though fearful it would be snatched at any moment. He stared hard at Kitty. The smallness of his beady eyes accentuated his nose and mouth, which subsequently appeared excessively large. His face and body were bony and angular and his lank hair hung down to his shoulders. He rested the ledger on a small table and took out a quill and ink from his pocket, contorting himself, crab-like, in order to write from a crouched position.

'Name?' he barked.

'Kitty Wilkinson.'

'From?'

'Beesthorpe Hall.'

He looked up from his ledger, obviously making the connection with the grisly story so much talked about in the locality.

'I have a letter from my employer, Mr. Bristowe.' Kitty handed it over and watched as his manner stiffened. When at last he spoke his face came uncomfortably close and she could see his spittle and smell his breath.

'A girl like you shouldn't be here – among decent folk. It ought to be the House of Correction for you – that's where whores go!'

'I'm not a whore, Sir.'

He thrust his face even closer. 'It says here you are. At least you are in my book and if it's like a whore you

110

behave, then it's like a whore you'll be treated. This is the workhouse and work you will.'

Kitty had retreated as he had advanced and now she was backed up against the wall. He looked at her closely and raised his hand to run his fingers slowly down her cheek, on to her neck and down to her chest. His breath came in rancid gasps as he leered over her.

'I'm in charge here, but I'm a fair man and you're a pretty little thing for sure. Maybe we can find a place for you here if you behave yourself. Mrs. Cartwright, see to our young inmate here. Make sure she settles in straight away Oh, and category two, if you please.'

Kitty was relieved when the Master picked up his ledger and left the room. She was trembling and in no doubt about the threat he presented to her. She would always have to be on her guard.

'Right. Bath house for you. Follow me.' Mrs. Cartwright marched out the door and across the yard to a small brick building. There was a central sunken area and tin baths were lined up with buckets of cold water next to them.

'Clothes off and thorough wash.' Mrs. Cartwright disappeared into a side room and came back with her arms full of clothing.

'You wear these from now on. I'll take everything of yours, if you please.'

She examined Kitty's slight body, looking for signs of anything contagious, and her eyes disapprovingly rested on the barely rounded stomach. When her fingers roughly searched her beautiful hair Kitty held her breath in case she cut it off, but she made do with the threat. 'You get lice and off it comes.'

'May I keep my boots?'

'No, you wear these clogs.'

Kitty put on the rough, grey dress, the tight cap and the unfamiliar clogs. The coarse material was stiff and itchy to her skin and the clogs were heavy.

'May I just keep my ribbons and hairbrush?' she asked timidly, but the rebuke came quickly.

'You keep nothing! Do you understand? Nothing!' Mrs. Cartwright snatched away the red ribbons in Kitty's hand.

'May I just ask one question? Please, what is category two?'

Mrs. Cartwright fixed Kitty with a resentful expression.

'Paupers like you cost a great deal of money to keep. Now some folks can't help falling on hard times – like their being sick an' all, or too old to work no more. They are the deserving poor and the gentry don't mind them so much. They look at it as their duty, see. But then the likes of you, whose misfortune is their own making through idleness, drink or bad behaviour – you're the undeserving poor, you are. Idle and profligate – Category two. And an unmarried woman with child is very undeserving indeed. It's a sin against man and God and you'll learn the wickedness of your ways here, my girl.'

As soon as Kitty stepped through the door to the workhouse itself, the smell hit her. Involuntarily, she put her hand to her mouth to try to prevent breathing in the heavy odour. What was it? She followed Mrs. Cartwright, keys jangling at her side, along the gloomy corridor, the unaccustomed clogs clapping on the hard floor. The small windows were very high up, so it was impossible to see out – just the endless painted brick walls. After negotiating a labyrinth of narrow corridors and heavy doors which clanged and echoed throughout the building, they came to the kitchen. Kitty realised that part of the pervading smell was emanating from here – a heavy, musty, odour that clung to the nostrils. There was also an overpowering smell of urine. The closets must be close by. Didn't they empty them?

'This is where you can work for now' Mrs. Cartwright was saying. 'Betty, show her how to scrub the pans. Then show her what to do for the top room and that can be her main task. Come on, girl!'

Betty smirked. Kitty stood rooted. An older woman, obviously in pain, hobbled awkwardly towards her.

'Hello, love. I'm Edith. You'll get used to it, don't you worry. Now you don't want to make her angry at the start, so you just pick up that pan and start scrubbing. There's a good girl.'

Kitty did as she was told. As she looked at the other women in the room, some returned her gaze dispassionately, some looked hostile and some just looked vacant, mindlessly toiling at their allotted task. Betty was the youngest, being about Kitty's age, but she was odd looking – loose mouthed and twitchy and one eye was badly infected. She had an unwell look to her, nourished but not healthy. In fact they all had that look – pale and pasty. No-one spoke. They just worked silently.

Kitty was grateful for Edith's words and advice. She washed and scrubbed and stacked tin plates for an hour or so and became very tired and thirsty. Two large cauldrons on the range bubbled under Edith's supervision and gave off a strong smell, unsurprisingly since the oatmeal she was adding to the milk and water was covered in a film of mould. Eventually, Edith started to ladle the contents of the pans into wooden bowls set out on trays.

'Come on, Betty. Show the new girl how to deal with the old ones.'

Betty offered a tray to Kitty. 'Take it. We've to go up and feed the old ones.'

'What is it?' Kitty asked, staring at the grey, glutinous mess in the tins.

'Gruel, of course!' The inference in the reply was that Kitty was obviously very stupid.

113

Kitty followed as they made their way up the steep staircases. The smell of urine was stronger than ever now, but nothing could have prepared Kitty for the stench when Betty opened the door of the top room. There were ten beds, five either side and each one contained an old, bedridden woman – or two. Some of the beds had double occupancy. A pathetic sound of moaning and pleading filled the room, although some lay inert and silent. At the sight of Kitty gasping and gagging, Betty smirked, but then relenting said 'Orrible, in't it. We change the straw in the mattresses tomorrow so it won't be so bad for a few days after that. Right. We feed them first and then we clean them up. Start spooning.'

Kitty had seen old, helpless women before, but none in this sickeningly pathetic state and not fifteen at a time. Nervously, she approached the first one. Little more than a skeleton, she made a high pitched noise as Kitty offered the first spoonful of gruel to her toothless mouth.

'Is she mad?' Kitty whispered.

'Oh yes.' replied Betty. 'They all are.'

They moved on down the line, spooning gruel into open mouths. Some wanted it and opened their mouths obediently, like little baby birds, while others clamped shut and turned their heads away in determined disgust.

At the end, by the high window, an old harridan sat and watched closely as the new girl made her way up the room. She fixed her stare on Kitty's face and as she approached the bed she shot out her hand, fingers bent like an old claw, and clamped tight on the young girl's arm. Startled and repulsed, Kitty tried to pull back, but the claw bit into her arm and would not release its victim.

Frightened now, Kitty looked at the woman for the first time. Thin white hair framed the bony face, and papery skin pulled tight over the cheekbones, descended into a cascade of scraggy wrinkles. The mouth formed a toothless, manic grin, but when Kitty looked into the eyes

114

she was surprised. They were hooded and watery with age but they were still blue and they reflected a wisdom and integrity along with a lively merriment. Was this a manifestation of her madness, Kitty wondered, but as if reading her thoughts, the old woman rasped 'That's right dearie. You look into old Bella's eyes to see into her soul. She's not so ugly on the inside. Not the same as the rest of her. Don't you be frightened of old Bella, pretty one. Now you leave that bowl to me. It's one thing I can do. See to the others.'

They took the bowls back to the kitchen and returned with wooden buckets full of cold water and some rags. The cleaning up process filled Kitty with horror but also compassion for the suffering of these miserable human beings. As the blankets were removed and the night shifts pulled up, most of them had purulent open sores.

'They mess themselves, see.' said Betty, scraping off the worst of the mess and then gently washing the skin. 'and their pee burns them, but like I said, we change the straw tomorrow.'

The ammonia stung their eyes and burned their nostrils but the two girls worked around the room and as they came to clean up Bella, her eyes turned to the sky beyond the high window.

'Won't be long before I'm there. High up in heaven with those fluffy, white clouds. Course I'll be an angel then and wipe my own backside.' Bella cackled with mirth at this thought and Kitty felt a little less frightened of her.

Back in the kitchen, Betty ladled out a bowl of gruel for each of them. While they had been toiling in the top ward, all the able bodied women and children had eaten at a long table, but now they had gone and the two girls were the last to eat.

'Sometimes it's good 'cos we get extra, but sometimes we go without when there's not enough left.' Betty explained.

Kitty looked down at her bowl and gingerly tasted the unappetizing contents. It was worse than she thought.

'It fills your belly. It's not always mouldy – just a bad sack of oats. Old Skinner got it cheap, I suppose. I'll have it if you don't want it.' Betty eagerly helped herself to Kitty's supper.

When the kitchen chores were finished, Kitty was shown the outside privy – a brick construction over a stinking open ditch. At last she was allowed to go to her bed. It was on the floor immediately beneath the old ones ward, laid out just the same with ten beds close together and one hook behind each bed on which to hang the workhouse clothes. The physical and mental status of the other inmates varied. Some were mentally defective and had known no other life, and some were decent women whom life had tossed away. All were bowed under the strain of poverty, discipline and deprivation.

Gratefully, Kitty sank on to the straw mattress. She was exhausted. The day had been endless. Was it just this morning she had set off from Beesthorpe Hall in bright sunshine? She thought of Mrs. Welby busy in the kitchen with her delicious pies and stews. She wanted to cry, to sob her heart out at the injustice of it all, but no tears came. She knew she would need all the willpower within her to get through this ordeal. There were no spare energies to waste on self-pity now. She lay in the darkness and prayed for herself and her baby.

CHAPTER THIRTEEN
George Skinner

THE morning came and so did the sickness. Kitty staggered outside to the privy. The ditch, which hadn't been cleared in ages, was revolting and the smell as well as the pregnancy made her vomit. Weak and trembling, she forced herself to follow Betty in the morning routine. She could not face the bowl of gruel herself and the sight of it being spooned into the old ones mouths made her heave yet again. She wondered what sort of a day it was outside but, only being able to see a small patch of sky visible through the high windows, she was unable to deduce much. As she reached the end of the ward and lifted her face to look longingly at the clouds, Bella's voice came to her.

'It's the worst thing, being shut in. That bit o' sky is all I got now. Me and my husband came in here together but he's dead now, God rest him. Not that I saw him once since we got through the door. We just said Goodbye. He went through the men's door and I came through the women's. Ain't no way I get down them stairs now 'cept in a box.'

Kitty glanced back at the old woman briefly and made no reply.

'Sometimes I wish I was mad like them. No-one to talk to here. That Betty's a poor little soul and as for the fat ugly one – she don't stay long in here I can tell you. Pokes her old head through the door looking just like an old bull-frog and hops off, quick as you like. Now you, you're a pretty face and we don't see many of your sort. We could be friends you and I. What's your name then?'

Kitty still stared at the sky and gave no indication that she was even listening to the old woman.

'Fallen on hard times have we?' Bella continued. 'Life's like that, love. My husband was a farm labourer out at Winkburn. My, he was handsome when he was young. Big and strong and worked all day. Had a cottage, we did. Course the wages was poor but we got by. We had children. They came pretty regular – and they died regular too.'

Kitty turned her face away from the window and looked back at Bella and the two women held each other's gaze for a few seconds. Bella knew she had hit on something but she could recognise trauma when she saw it. Time. That was what this girl needed.

Kitty was relieved that the next meal at least was not gruel. It was a portion of rough bread and a tiny amount of cheese. Edith had warmed up some milk and water and ladled it over the old ones bowls to make a sop, their toothless gums being unable to cope with the hard bread.

'Tomorrow's Sunday.' Edith said conspiratorially. 'That means suet pudding and potatoes! Course we don't get as much as the men but we do get a bit. Something for you to look forward to, love.'

Kitty tried to smile her appreciation for the encouraging words but made no reply. Her spirits were so low and her pregnancy made her feel so ill, she had nothing to spare for talking but she liked Edith. Edith wasn't really old but her feet were deformed and she could do little more than hobble a few steps, so she mainly stood by the range chopping, stirring and ladling. She knew that she would do that for the rest of her life. Edith knew that the young girl found it hard to be here and until her spirit was crushed and she accepted the monotonous routine, all she could offer her were a few kind words. Mrs. Cartwright suddenly appeared and the atmosphere changed. 'Bella's right.' Kitty thought, 'she does look like a bullfrog.'

'Mr. Skinner wants to see you – Mr. Skinner, the Master. Up the first stairs and it's the door on the left. Knock first.'

'I have to take the bowls up to the old ones.'

'You have to see Mr. Skinner. That's what you have to do when you're told.'

George Skinner stood in the centre of an oval-shaped room, nicely furnished with drapes, a carpet and a fireplace. Kitty thought it odd to find a room like that amidst such a spartan, prison-like building. He was not a big man and his weasely eyes, thin side-whiskers and odious manner made Kitty inwardly recoil as she stood before him.

'Ah, Miss Wilkinson.' he began mockingly. 'I see you have settled in.' He advanced and put his hand on Kitty's upper arm. 'Warming to your tasks, are you? Top floor isn't it? Not easy, I'm sure but they have to be cared for and we can't expect decent women to do the task when the likes of you are here.' The parody of concern was nothing more than gloating patronisation as his eyes greedily explored her face and body. Kitty froze.

'Now, we could come to an arrangement, you and I. I could make life a little easier for you and you, of course, could co-operate with me in a number of ways.' His hand travelled down to her hips and Kitty tried to wrench herself free.

'Don't act the pure maiden with me, Missy. It's not as if it's something you're not used to, now is it? He pulled her closer to him and breathed heavily 'No-one would know. It would be just you and I – our secret.' His fingers began to pull up the skirt of her dress.

Revulsion overcame her and suddenly, with vehemence, Kitty found her voice. 'No! It would not be a secret! I would tell everybody and make no mistake Reverend Becher would get to hear of it. You will not touch me!' she spat. The unexpected outburst took

Skinner aback and Kitty used the advantage of the moment to turn and run from the room. Her clogs rattled on the stairs as she hurtled down to the sanctuary of the kitchen. She burst through the door and closed it defensively behind her, leaning against it and breathing heavily. Mrs. Cartwright and everyone in the room looked up. In the midst of their tasks they stopped and stared but not a word was spoken.

Kitty was barely able to summon the strength to carry the tray up to the top room and start spooning the bread and milk. 'What had she done now? Would anyone ever believe her if Skinner took revenge on her. She knew a committee met regularly at the workhouse. It would always be possible to get word somehow, wouldn't it?'

Bella watched Kitty's face closely as she worked her way up the room. She could see the variety of emotions playing on the pretty face – worry, disgust, doubt and panic. Bella missed nothing. Back in the kitchen, Kitty managed to eat the bread and drink some milk and water and took strength from it. She needed it. As Betty had promised, the straw pallets were to be changed.

One at a time, they lugged up the stairs a clean straw mattress. The two of them rolled the occupant and removed the soiled one. What a smell they stirred up! The sodden, soiled mattress had to be manhandled down the stairs, the cover removed and the contents piled up outside to dry and then be burned or dug into the garden. It was exhausting and a very long job. As they were moved the old ones wailed piteously with the pain of their sores and Kitty tried to soothe them. However, Betty's prediction proved to be correct and the air in the room became much cleaner, perfumed by the fresh, sweet straw.

Sunday came and there was no respite in Kitty's workload but at half past ten every able-bodied inmate congregated in the committee room on the ground floor. They stood close together in rows and for the first time Kitty saw the men. There weren't many of them, mostly being young boys or old men with perhaps a limb missing or some other mental or physical affliction. It was a sorry gathering.

Rev. Becher took the service. He was a handsome gentleman, if a little overweight, but he had a kindly manner and an imposing presence and his sermon was easy to listen to and understand. He talked about sin and forgiveness and Kitty even took slight comfort from his words. Perhaps God would forgive her after all, even if society didn't. The hymns were the simple well known ones but the prayers were harder to follow and seemed to go on an extraordinarily long time. Kitty's knees hurt as she kneeled on the hard floor for the prayers, yet when she stood for the sermon she felt light headed and faint. Eventually the service concluded and she turned with the others to file out the door. An arm reached out to detain her. Rev. Becher had crossed the room and now looked directly at her.

'You must be Kitty Wilkinson. Mr. Bristowe told me of your plight.' He lead Kitty to the side of the room in a show of privacy. 'I hope you are settling in?'

'Yes, Sir. Thank you Sir.'

George Skinner had sidled up behind the Rev. Becher, his loathsome face imposing itself on Kitty's line of vision as she replied to the kindly Reverend, who now continued 'Mr. Bristowe asked me to keep an eye on your wellbeing and I have promised him so to do. Is all well with you here? Do you have any concerns regarding your situation?'

Kitty allowed her eyes to rest fully on Skinner. His face changed as the implication of the question dawned on him.

'There is a concern, Sir. I fear it is a serious one, otherwise I should not trouble you.' Skinner narrowed his flinty eyes threateningly as beads of perspiration broke out on his face. Kitty looked at him steadily and enjoyed the power of the moment.

'Speak on, child.' the Reverend encouraged. 'Speak on.'

'Well, Sir' Kitty took a deep breath and resolutely proceeded. 'It's the old ones. I have been consigned to care for them, the bedridden ones. They have sores on them, caused by the inconvenience of their bodily functions and we have no salve to apply for their ease. It seems to me if this were provided, much pain and misery could be avoided.'

Relief flooded through Skinner but the Reverend remained unaware even of his presence. He stared at Kitty and finally smiled as he said 'Jesus Christ teaches us to think of others before ourselves, as you have done. God has provided the repentant sinner – and I shall provide the salve!'

Rev. Becher threw back his head and laughed and with a swish of his clerical cloak, made his exit. Kitty allowed herself one glance at Skinner before retreating. In that fleeting space of time they both knew that from now on, with the Rev. Becher as her protector, Kitty was safe and George Skinner would leave her alone.

CHAPTER FOURTEEN
Bella

THE long awaited suet pudding ration arrived. 'There's no point in putting any in the old ones' bowls – they wouldn't be able to eat it, what with no teeth an' all.' Edith explained. 'Better they have the bread and milk. Bit more for us then, dear.' The puddings had boiled in the bubbling pans all morning and Kitty was eager to catch a glimpse of the precious luxury as Edith reverently untied and cut them into portions, allocating one lump per bowl. She had imagined that it would be similar to Mrs. Welby's hearty suet pudding but when she tried it she realised that the allocation of suet was meagre and it was just a tasteless, leaden lump.

'We wait all week for that?' Kitty was bitterly disappointed. She could not believe that something so horrible could be the highlight of her culinary fare from now on. Edith's kindly manner turned a little sharp as she replied 'It's all you'll get so be grateful and mind you eat it.'

Up in the top room Bella chattered away as Kitty worked her way towards her. 'I heard the singing. Hymns do a power of good for the soul, don't you think, Kitty? It is Kitty isn't it? I heard Betty call you that. She don't come so often now, does she? She'll be happy to leave all this work to you now.'

As Kitty bent over the old woman, a blonde curl escaped from the workhouse cap and fell down like a golden spring. Bella gasped and reaching out her bony hand, held the curl lovingly between her bent old fingers. Kitty resisted the temptation to pull her head away and retrieve her hair as the wizened old woman clucked and crooned over the beauty of it.

'What a sight for sore old eyes that is.' she whispered. Gently, she reached up and pulled the work cap from Kitty's head. Her hair cascaded down in tumbling waves and Bella's eyes were soft as she tenderly caressed the mass of curls. 'You're a lovely girl and no mistake. Like a precious little bird in an ugly cage. You should be free, where the sun shines, strolling with your young man perhaps.'

Kitty retrieved her cap, stuffed her protesting hair back under it and worked her way back up the room, comforting and cajoling where necessary. Bella watched her and said to herself quietly 'One day, my lovely, you'll tell old Bella your story. One day before too long.'

In the workhouse there was no sense of time – just the endless daily grind of sameness and toil and the luxury of bone weary sleep. It was a strictly disciplined regime full of petty rules designed to constantly remind the inmate of their lowly status. The rations, though excrutiatingly monotonous, sustained life and filled stomachs. The lives of the men and women remained strictly segregated, with women in the west wing, men in the east and children in rooms at the back. Families were heartlessly split up, only coming together for the Sunday service. The children did play together and even received some education in a room set aside for schooling but the exercise yards were separate for the different sexes. Surrounded by a high wall, making it impossible to see anything other than tree tops and sky, the women would shuffle round, gulping in the fresh air and revelling in any small degree of sunshine to fall on their faces.

After a while Kitty actually found the daily routine no hardship. In fact it helped to heal the mental scars, there now being in her life no yesterday and no tomorrow – just more days the same as today. She didn't even think about the hard work after a few weeks, adapting as she did to the restrictions of her enclosed world. The sickness started to ease and beneath the rough workhouse dress she became aware of the changes in her body. Her little stomach became hard and round and whereas she actually became thinner, the belly slowly grew.

Over the weeks another gradual but astounding change came about. In Kitty's new life she became fiercely protective and devoted to the care of the old ones. They were her salvation and she worked hard to bring a touch of humanity and comfort into their lives as they slowly rotted in their beds. Rev. Becher, true to his word, had provided the salve and she applied it carefully and with tenderness.

As the autumn rolled on and the weather turned colder, Kitty boldly asked Rev. Becher for extra blankets for her charges. She ignored Skinner's warning looks as she approached one Sunday to make her plea, and the following week extra blankets duly arrived. Even so, the old ones started to die, mostly in the night and after prolonged chest rattling. Sometimes Kitty would sit with them if she felt they could appreciate some comfort but as they slipped further into the arms of death she would have to leave to seek her own rest. She would return in the morning to find the body cold and stiff. Albert and Fred, the two able bodied men who generally worked in the garden, would appear with a large canvass, roll the body into it and awkwardly negotiate the stairs down to the ground floor. They would cross the yard and deposit the body onto a slab in the mortuary. If no relative came to claim it, a crude coffin would be constructed and it would be taken down to the Southwell cemetary where a cleric would give the funeral service in as short a time as possible. As the cold earth closed in over the coffin it denied to the world forever that this pauper in an unmarked grave had ever been warm and loving – a daughter, a niece, a wife or a mother.

Kitty's revulsion at her first sight of these pathetic old women had disappeared completely. She now failed to see them as dried up, crazed old creatures who had lived beyond their usefulness. As she worked, feeding and cleaning them, she knew that once they had been wholesome, good natured and caring. That they had come to this helplessness in their extreme old age was not their fault. Poverty, as well as infirmity, could not be helped and Kitty cared for her old ones with great devotion.

And Bella. What part did she play in this awakening of Kitty's soul? Bella's part was crucial because she was the voice for them all. Day by day she gave Kitty glimpses of her youth, her childhood, her love of her husband, her modest home and garden and her much mourned dead babies. Bella had a way with words and gradually she painted the picture and sprinkled it with humour and anecdotes so that she became for Kitty that young vigorous woman, full of life and learning to cope with all the trials besetting her. Through Bella, Kitty realised that the other women would tell a similar tale if they could. They hadn't always been mad old harridans.

Kitty still didn't talk much herself but she liked to listen to the old woman and had begun to enjoy her company. Though Bella's body was giving up on her, her eyesight and mind remained sharp, and one morning she realised the reason for Kitty's changing appearance. She put out her hand and laid it upon the now protruding belly, well hidden under the heavy workhouse dress.

'How far gone do you think?'

'Six months or so.'

'Perhaps it's time to tell old Bella the story. Nothing can shock me, dearie. You heard my stories enough times these last weeks. Now it's time to tell yours.'

Reluctantly at first, Kitty started the story. Hesitantly she related the sequence of events, putting into words for the first time the trauma of that catastrophic night. There were frequent silences when she just could not bring herself to say the words. The regret, the loss and the pain were almost too much to bear – so much easier to lock it away in her mind rather than face the guilt directly, but Bella waited patiently for the words to come, never showing any reaction to the tragic revelations. When finally Kitty had finished, the old woman reached out and caressed her arm. Gradually, she enfolded her and Kitty sank gratefully into the bony embrace. Just like a mother, Bella stroked her while she cried. As the tears subsided she took up a positive, hopeful viewpoint.

'A baby, Kitty. After all you've suffered, now you are to be favoured with the best gift of all – a baby! I can think of no better ending for your sad tale, even though it brought you here. All will be well, child. Take heart.' But when Kitty left the top room Bella turned her troubled face to the window and her bit of sky. She prayed for her young friend and her unborn child, knowing the difficulties that lay ahead, but most of all she remembered the feared prophecy of doom for the child of the workhouse. The legacy of a child born in the workhouse was grim enough. After all, how much more disadvantaged was it possible to be? But there was more to it than that. The prediction known locally was harsh and uncompromising. It foretold of a damned destiny. Only bad will come to the child born of the workhouse. Only bad.

The weeks crept by and winter's grip took hold. Thick frost formed on the inside of the windows, blocking out even Bella's bit of sky. In the unheated rooms cheeks were pinched and blue, noses ran and hands were red and painful. Inmates lived in a fog of their own expelled breath. Breaking the ice on a bowl of water before washing and shivering in the privy became the daily endurance. Hacking coughs constantly reverberated around the building. The kitchen was the only warm place and everyone made an excuse to visit it and stay as long as possible, warming themselves by the stove. Kitty grew more exhausted by the day and it showed on her gaunt face. There was no let up in her daily schedule – no exception made for her because of her condition. Betty had been assigned to other duties and now helped only with changing the mattresses, a revolting but necessary chore but one which temporarily transformed the top room into one fit for human habitation.

In the bitter cold, the old ones died with chilling regularity. It was a trauma for them to wake up to find a corpse lying in the same bed. New inmates would arrive, some lasting only a matter of weeks before they too gave up the struggle for their miserable existence. Occasionally there would be a little time to spare and Kitty would sit on Bella's bed, speculating on life beyond the high, frosted windows. Sometimes she combed the thin white hair or gently warmed the frail old hands with her own but always they chatted, as friends do, of events past and present and, of course the future. Or rather, Kitty's future. They had become soulmates and Bella tried hard to provide a glimmer of hope to which the young girl could cling.

'What will it be like, Bella? The birthing?'

'Well, my love, labour is what they calls it and labour it surely is. You'll feel your body is fit to break in two but you keep on pushing because when that baby comes and you first set your eyes on it – well, it'll be the best moment of your life. You keep that thought in your head as you labour on child, but you mind one thing more' Bella wagged a finger at Kitty in mock severity 'As soon as you can, you bring that baby up for me to see. You and your lovechild have given me a reason to live and for that I'm grateful. I pray that God will allow you to keep your baby and not take him up to the angels like he did all mine.'

Excitement grew within the workhouse when news came that on Christmas Eve there was to be a party. A party! Imagine! At the appointed time all the inmates, scrubbed up and self-conscious, trooped into the committee room. A table was set out with pies and cider. Rev. Becher made a little speech telling them that they must all be grateful for this benevolence bestowed upon them by the good people of Southwell. There were three ladies present and Kitty realised she had forgotten how beautiful dresses could be with their frilled edges and satin bows. She felt awkward with her ungainly body and ugly dress and cap but the ladies were gracious and after the pies had been eaten and the cider drunk they gave each child a present. The carved wooden toys were crude but their magic worked as the faces of the children were transfixed with wonder. The men received a ration of tobacco. Blind man's buff was played and the room rang with unaccustomed laughter. A Miss Pringle was introduced and she sat down at the piano and played the Christmas hymns. Afterwards she played jolly tunes and the songs became more boisterous with 'Oh Dear What Can The Matter Be' and 'Hearts of Oak'.

Eventually the party was over. A small window of time in their tedious lives had closed but it had provided the gift of a precious memory, to be re-lived at will. Kitty felt flushed with pleasure. She was grateful to Miss Pringle for her joyous piano playing, but the party had given her more than enjoyment. For the first time since the tragedy she felt peace of mind and hope for the future. Perhaps she was a little intoxicated from the cider or the sound of her own laughter but she felt happy and so she hurried, as fast as her awkward bulk would allow, up to the top room to tell Bella all about it

The old woman listened closely to every detail, chuckling at Kitty's descriptions and seeing it all in her mind. When she had finished Bella reached behind her and brought out something in her hand.

'I have a present for you, Kitty.'

'A present? For me?'

'Well, for the baby.' She opened her palm and there lay a small brown hazelnut. It had a hole through it and was threaded on to a piece of red ribbon.

'It's for you to give to the baby. A token of your love.'

Kitty held up the hazelnut and fingered the red ribbon in wonder.

'Yes, Kitty, my love.' Bella's voice was soft. 'It is Jeremiah's ribbon. The one that he gave you that day in Newark.'

Kitty's eyes brimmed and a lump came to her throat. She was unable to ask how this miracle had come to happen. The red ribbon represented joy and life – gifts now lost to her in her colourless world. The image of that wonderful Sunday swam before her eyes. She could almost feel Jeremiah as she envisaged the moment when, side by side coming home on the carriage, he had taken her hand in his. The small gift had moved her beyond words and she kissed the old woman's cheek.

After she had gone, Bella reflected on what she had omitted to tell Kitty. She had sent word for Mrs. Cartwright and had pleaded for this small favour. It was the custom of the workhouse. There being a strong chance that the mother would die in childbirth, the giving of the hazelnut to the child as a token of the love it would never know, was very poignant. Mrs. Cartwright had reluctantly agreed to perform this small task and, ignorant of the emotional importance, had used one of Kitty's red ribbons.

Bella prayed that it would be Kitty's face the child would look to for love in the years to come and not the hazelnut token.

CHAPTER FIFTEEN
The Baby

KITTY'S puny little body tenaciously held and nurtured the growing baby inside her and, against all odds, she carried the child almost to full term. The relationship between Kitty and Bella had grown into something very special. They both needed and depended on each other for companionship and whereas Bella relied on her young friend to remind her of the vigour of life, now lost to her, so Kitty needed the old woman's sensible and encouraging advice to sustain her through her ordeal. Bella prayed that the poor girl would survive the birth and the prophecy would be wrong.

It was a bitter cold February night when Kitty went into labour. Mrs. Cartwright was sent for and she ushered the frightened girl into a separate sick room. With stabbing pains gripping her, Kitty staggered into the cold, bare room and collapsed on the hard pallet. As the pains increased in intensity and the contractions wracked her body, Mrs. Cartwright's harsh attitude softened a little and she tried her best to soothe her. In kindly tones for once she said 'Everything will be alright. The midwife has been sent for.' She mopped Kitty's face and patted her encouragingly.

Eventually, the door opened and the midwife, well wrapped against the cold night and carrying a brown cloth bag, bustled purposefully into the room. She removed her cloak to reveal a filthy apron. 'Well, now what have we here? A few more candles if you please Mrs. Cartwright.' Muttering under her breath about the cost of candles, Mrs. Cartwright set them up and the midwife lifted Kitty's shift.

131

'A long way to go yet, I declare.' she pronounced.

The pains grew worse and when they came Kitty cried out and thrashed around the bed, unable to bear the agony. The long winter's night wore slowly on with Kitty trying desperately to push the reluctant baby out into the world. In the brief respite between pains she lay in the flickering candlelight, wild-eyed with fear at this abominable experience. She wanted to get up and run away – even Bella's instructions had not prepared her for this. The midwife did little to help but Mrs. Cartwright continued to mop and soothe the suffering girl. She couldn't help but think of the last two births in the workhouse. In both cases mother and child had died. She realised that she had come to be quite fond of Kitty. She had shown herself to be a good worker and had not given them any trouble. It would be a shame if she died now in childbirth but of course, it happened all the time. Her new-found compassion moved her to question the midwife. 'Is there anything else we can do? Should we call a doctor? There's a new one in Southwell – He's young and I hear he's quite good.'

The midwife shook her head. She seemed impervious to Kitty's cries. She'd seen it all so many times before and it showed on her hard face. 'You can never tell how a birthing will go. Some get on with it and pop them out no trouble. Others go on for days. She could be one of those.'

With her grubby hands, she probed into Kitty to try to find the cause of the slow delivery.'Stuck to her back.' she declared. 'Not going to move without this.' She held up a fearsome, rusty hook. 'It's a case for the crochet. The question is – where to place it without taking the child's eye out?' The midwife hovered over the helpless girl with the hateful instrument at the ready but Kitty, had heard her words. 'No!' she screamed. 'Please don't do anything to hurt my baby. Please don't. Please. No. No.' She thrashed her head from side to side as she pleaded and endeavoured to push even harder.

'Perhaps we should wait a while before resorting to that' Mrs. Cartwright reasoned. ' Don't touch the girl with the hook. Do you hear me? I'm going to see about sending for a doctor.' and she hastened away to ask permission of Mr. Skinner for the doctor to be summoned.

George Skinner, roused from sleep by the urgent knocking, peered into Mrs. Cartwright's face as she spoke urgently. The candlelight sent sinister shadows over him as he struggled to follow her words. 'The girl is not doing well and the baby is wedged. May I send to town for the doctor?'

Skinner narrowed his eyes and then exclaimed in disbelief. 'A doctor! Have you taken leave of your senses, Mrs. Cartwright? A doctor would have to be paid. I fear the girl is not worth the expense.'

'But Mr. Skinner, Sir. The midwife is unable to help except to use her hook and you know what that means. It would be too cruel.'

'And no less than she deserves. Besides, budget, Mrs. Cartwright, budget. If we spend money on doctor's bills, we must cut back on some other necessity – food perhaps. Tell the girl she must do this herself. And remember ' he said pompously, 'it is written in the Bible 'In sorrow thou shalt bring forth children.' and he shut the door.

Mrs. Cartwright made her way back through the ice-cold corridors to the sick room. Kitty was gripped in a vice of pain and her shrieks were heart rending. The midwife shook her head.

'No progress.' she said flatly. She inclined her head towards the hook in an unmistakable gesture that it must be used soon.

High up in the top room Bella heard Kitty's screams and suffered with her. Through the window she could see the full moon with a halo of frost encircling it and even her dim old eyes could make out hundreds of stars glittering like diamonds in the black sky. She pulled the blanket up to her chin and anxiously plucked at it with her gnarled old fingers, mouthing silent prayers.

The dark hours wore on and Kitty became weaker. Her curls were congealed with sweat and plastered to her head. Mrs. Cartwright knocked once more on Mr. Skinner's door and once more he refused permission for the doctor to be called.

'But, Sir, I fear she may die. It's just like the others.' The door slammed in her face.

'I'm going out.' she said to the midwife on her return. 'If you as much as touch that girl with your filthy hook, you will not be paid one penny. Do you understand that?' The midwife sniffed and folded her arms defensively.

As the cold light of dawn broke across the sky Mrs. Cartwright put on her cloak and bonnet and slipped quietly out of the workhouse. The frost was so hard that her breath seemed to freeze in her lungs and she pulled her cloak tighter to her, quickening her pace. Guilt spurred her on. She should have done this hours ago. Thoughts of the tragic way the other births had ended filled her mind. George Skinner was a heartless man and she knew why he was taking this out on Kitty. The agonized face of the young girl swam before her eyes – misery she was used to but this was cruel suffering. She would pay for the doctor herself if need be but she could stand by no longer, God's will or not.

She hurried down the lane and crossed the bridge by the mill. The bare branches of the willows, festooned with thick rime, hung low over the pathway and she brushed past them, taking the direct route on up to the town. Puffed out and gasping, she knocked on the doctor's door, sending the urgent rapping of the knocker echoing down the deserted street.

Young Dr. Prentiss appeared in his dressing gown. Breathlessly, Mrs. Cartwright asked for his help. 'A birthing? At the workhouse you say. Why, of course.' He retreated to dress and within minutes was pulling on his coat and closing the door even before Mrs. Cartwright had caught her breath. 'Lead on.' he said, snatching up his bag and striding off down the street. She was immediately left behind so she called to him 'Go in the side door, first corridor, third door on the left.'

Dr. Prentiss saluted recognition of the instructions and lengthened his stride still further.

'Ah, the same old smell of the workhouse' he said to himself as the door closed behind him. First light was seeping into the corridor as he found his way and entered the sick room. The sight of the young girl, ravaged by the trauma of the hideous birth pains, exhausted yet still straining, moved him and he addressed the midwife brusquely. He observed her filthy clothes and hands and when he caught sight of the vicious hook he was outraged. 'Put that away and stay clear.' He ordered. She cast him a resentful look but knew better than to object and backed quietly to the side of the room.

Dr. Prentiss took off his jacket and rolled up his sleeves. 'The baby is wedged and time is running out for both of them.' Mrs. Cartwright puffed into the room in time to be ordered out to fetch clean water and rags. Weak now, but still moaning pitifully, Kitty had little strength left to push but still she tried. 'Hush, child. I am here to help you. We must be calm and all will be well.' He took from his bag a small bottle and held it to her lips. 'This will help the pain and also help ease the baby out.' he said. The laudenum trickled down Kitty's throat. Her imploring eyes reached deep into his soul as he held her head and tried to reassure her.

As she drifted off into a stupour, the doctor washed her carefully, soothed her brow and waited. 'The baby

135

has a better chance of coming now that she is relaxed and calm.' he said to the two women. He was helpless to do anything further to aid mother and child but he had seen the grotesque results of the use of the midwife's hook and was determined that it would never be used in his presence again.

After some time, he realised that the baby was indeed making progress and he worked to ease its final stage of delivery into the world. Dr. Prentiss held up the pitiful scrap of humanity. It was a bluish colour and did not cry. He handed it to the midwife and turned his attention to Kitty as she began to bleed profusely. He was powerless to stop the flow and the bright red blood gushing from her contrasted starkly with her chalk white face. Her whimperings grew faint and her skin turned cold. The doctor felt angry and helpless. He tried to remain dispassionate, as he had been trained, but it was difficult and he found himself stroking the matted hair of the dying girl. Just once she opened her eyes and looked for her baby but as she did so her pulse slowed and her breath left her for the very last time. She had never even gazed upon her child – Jeremiah's child. The doctor closed her eyes and touched her white face tenderly with the back of his hand. He whispered wearily 'God keep you safe. May you rest in peace.'

Behind him, the midwife had taken charge of the baby. She wrapped it carefully, put it in a box and waited for it to die. Sadly, Mrs. Cartwright walked across the room and looked down at the pathetic child. After a few moments she remembered something and searched in her pocket. Gently she placed the hazelnut with the red ribbon beside the baby.

Dr. Prentiss breathed deeply of the frosty morning air as he walked home with a heavy heart. He hoped that one day he would become immune to the suffering and sadness that accompanied his profession but he feared he never would. Bella lay watching her bit of sky, tears working their way down her wrinkled face as she mourned her young friend. 'God can take me now.' she mumbled to herself. 'Only bad will come of it now. Only bad.'

Kitty was buried in an unmarked, pauper's grave in Southwell before nightfall.

CHAPTER SIXTEEN
The Rev. Cuthbert Birtwistle

1875

S O it was over fifty years after Kitty's tragic death that Wilhelmina, Richard and Cook sat in the kitchen at Beesthorpe Hall and discussed what the day would bring. 'An exorcism. What do you reckon that is exactly then?' Richard asked.

'I think it's like summoning the evil spirit and then sending it on its way. To where it's supposed to be. That'll be heaven, I suppose.' mused Cook.

Wilhelmina shuddered. 'Or hell. You wouldn't want the spirit of the thing that I saw in heaven. I wonder what did happen in that locked room, all those years ago? Nobody seems to know.'

'Well' said Richard cautiously. I spoke to Jed about it a bit. He couldn't remember much but I think it was an affair of the heart. Jealousy – that sort of thing. Someone died.' He hoped his deliberate vagueness would convince them that he knew no more. The fact was that Jed's story had had a profound effect on Richard. He had found himself going into the wash-house and imagining the two bodies there. He had even gone up to the attic to stand looking at the door, trying to picture it all. The truth was that it was a very disturbing story and he didn't want to upset Wilhelmina by relating it. She worked in the wash-house. If she knew what had happened there – she might leave. He didn't want that.

Cook put down her cup and saucer and heaved herself out of her chair. 'Well, that's the last respite I'll have all day. Luncheon to prepare but no-one can tell me for what time. Mrs. Pollard says they don't know how long it will take. Could be all day but the Bishop's man likes his food so I've to have it ready. Did you bring me those potatoes, Richard?'

'Just outside the door. I'll get them.' Richard brought in a basket full of small white potatoes with fresh earth clinging to them. At the side was a bunch of carrots with their feathery tops just beginning to wilt. Cook smiled in appreciation. She was happy to leave spiritual matters to spiritual people. She would do what she did best.

'Come along Winnie. Work will take our minds off the goings-on.'

'I'll be back soon.' Richard said as he disappeared through the door. 'Captain Pollard has asked me to be on hand.' He could have added that he would rather be anywhere than in the house whilst this ceremony took place but it didn't sound very brave, even to himself, so he didn't. He whistled as usual as he returned to the garden.

At eight o'clock that morning in Southwell Minster, the Rev. Birtwistle rose stiffly from his knees. For two hours he had prayed at the altar in preparation for the task which lay ahead of him that day. As the diocesan exorcist, appointed by the Bishop of Southwell, he relied on the supremacy of good over evil and as he, the representative of the Church, would confront the evil force, so he must be cleansed of all sin. His prolonged devotions were in order to achieve a piety of spirit robust enough to conquer the devil himself.

Rev. Birtwistle was acknowledged to be an expert in this field and had indeed brought about some successful dispatches of unwanted spirits – those lost souls unable or unwilling to move on to the next world. They were mostly harmless, lost spirits. He preferred to think of himself as performing a ministry of deliverance, of ushering these spirits on to the care of God with prayer and commands in the Name of Christ Almighty. It was

139

sometimes an exhausting experience for him, depending on the resistance of the spirit, and he was no longer a young man. The extensive prayers took their toll on his knees and his back.

As he left the Minster by the side door and crossed the churchyard back to Vicars Court, where he had lived all his life, he tried to convince himself he wasn't really hungry. In accordance with Jesus' teaching, not only prayer but fasting was required prior to casting out of spirits and, in truth, his stomach protested more than his knees. His short, corpulent frame bore witness to his healthy appetite and his housekeeper's attention to her duty, but this morning he would go without his usual hearty breakfast. He had, however, dined well the previous evening. His housekeeper had excelled herself and laden the dining table with great tureens of roast chicken and vegetables. The dark wine had glowed ruby red in the crystal goblet as he held it up against the fire-light and his contentment with life was as large as his appetite.

But this morning, in order to be ready for the task ahead, he must put all thought of sustenance out of his mind. The Bishop's elegant carriage, pulled by two matched bays, was already outside, waiting to take him to the place of the day's work. He regarded the honour of the use of this conveyance not only as a token of esteem for his work, but as a small recompense for the inconvenience to his person, which was not inconsiderable given the mental and physical hardships sometimes involved.

The housekeeper, at a loss with no breakfast to prepare, fussed over the Reverend like a mother hen. She handed him his black cloak and hat, freshly brushed, and hovered as he checked the contents of his bag, already packed with the accoutrements necessary for the work ahead. With a cheery 'I shall return before nightfall' he left the house and approached the awaiting carriage. He paused briefly, as he always did, to admire the magnificent horses and stroke their velvet muzzles. The morning being pleasant, his cloak lay lightly on his shoulders and in a sudden breeze flapped gaily behind him. The horses reared their heads and snorted, their eyes wild until the coachman steadied them.

'Onward to Beesthorpe, coachman.' said the Reverend heartily. 'At a goodly pace, if you please.'

Rev. Birtwistle settled himself back in the carriage and prepared to enjoy the passing countryside in the May sunshine. To his knowledge he had never been to Beesthorpe before but was told it lay near to the village of Caunton and that an elegant, Elizabethan mansion was their destination. He couldn't help hoping that it would prove to be an easy assignment, just a simple wilful spirit that wouldn't take too much out of him. Then afterwards he could appreciate the luncheon to which he had been invited to stay. He hoped it would be prepared by a cook who knew her stuff – one never knew what to expect in the country.

The pleasant journey passed quickly enough and on poking his head out of the carriage to enquire how much longer, Rev. Birtwistle was informed by the coachman that Beesthorpe Hall lay directly ahead. He craned his neck further and through the trees he did indeed see a beautiful house. The full morning sun bathed it in a rich, golden light and glinted and sparkled off the window panes and chimney pots. The carriage continued on up the drive, past a modest lake and through the wooded parkland. 'Very agreeable' he thought to himself. 'If only the cook is up to standard.'

Captain Pollard paced up and down in the drawing room, constantly looking up the drive for the arrival of both the Bishop's man and the agent.

'Do try to stay calm, Edward.' Mrs. Pollard pleaded. 'If this is going to placate the servants then all well and good. I've spoken to Cook and asked her to prepare a luncheon that will keep warm for an indefinite time. Not that anything much will happen, I am quite sure. At least this is not a service for which we are having to pay.'

'I've asked Richard to be on hand. Just in case of any, er – difficulties. There's no sign of a carriage.' Captain Pollard peered out. He actually agreed with his wife, for once. The whole thing was ridiculous. But part of him found it rather unnerving – the unknown, he supposed. 'Ah. I see it coming now.'

The sweating horses slowed to enter the gates and negotiate the circular drive to pull up in front of the house. The carriage wheels crunched to a halt. Rev. Birtwistle composed himself for a moment and then opened the door to alight. A puzzled look came over him as he stared up at the house. From the distance the house had been bright, shining and welcoming but now, viewed closely, it was sombre and brooding and partly covered in thick ivy as though hiding its face from the world. A dark cloud passed in front of the sun, the air became chill and the light dulled. A sudden wind sprang up and the ivy, rampant right up to the attic windows, whispered menacingly. The chill penetrated the Reverend's cloak and a strong feeling of foreboding passed right through him as he stood stock still by the carriage.

'Captain Pollard, at your service, Sir.' Whilst the Reverend's attention had been taken by the house, the door had opened and now standing before him was a tall gentleman in a slightly agitated state. He offered his hand and then turned saying 'Come in. Come in.'

'Thank you but no.' said Reverend Birtwistle.

Captain Pollard was, to say the least, surprised at the response to his invitation to enter the house and looked at his guest enquiringly.

142

'I was given to understand that Mr. Smith-Woolley would accompany me this morning.' continued the Reverend. 'Do I take it that he has not yet arrived?'

'That is correct. Being the land agent for this estate, he has possession of the key to the room in question but I assure you he is expected at any moment.'

'I am aquainted with Mr. Smith-Woolley and know him to be a devoutly religious man. His presence will be needed. We will await his arrival.'

Captain Pollard was still perplexed by this hold up of the proceedings. 'Shall we not just step inside, Reverend. There may be rain.'

'In that event we shall shelter in the carriage. I shall not cross the threshold of this unhappy house without a Godly man at my side.' The Reverend's tone was resolute and final.

'Ah. Quite so.' Captain Pollard tried not to feel hurt that he alone was not sufficient support for the portly cleric. He was, after all, a Christian himself but plainly he did not count. He looked back up the drive, willing the carriage to come and relieve him of the sole responsibility of this sombre little man sent by the Bishop of Southwell.

There was relief all around when the trap driven by Mr. Smith-Woolley, clattered down the drive. Barely had the foreward momentum of the cart ceased before he leapt to the ground and bounded towards the two men standing awkwardly together before the house.

'Good morning, gentlemen. And a fine morning it is for our task, is it not?'

Cecil Smith-Woolley enjoyed a rumbustious good humour and an exuberant love of life but this seemingly superficial exterior masked the man beneath. Rev. Birtwistle was glad to see his friend. He could ask for no better man to accompany him today, for the successful exorcist must be selfless in his dedication to God and to the good of others. Cecil Smith-Woolley hit the mark on both counts. At this moment though, with mock concern, he felt in his pockets and, as if for the entertainment of a delighted crowd, produced the key to the locked room with a theatrical flourish.

'This key has been in my office since the day I started working. My father told me only that it was the key to a tragedy, long since forgotten. Now the day has come to discover it.' His face was flushed with excitement and expectation.

Rev. Birtwistle was, however, unimpressed with the timing of this flippant attitude and took control of the situation by speaking with gravity. 'I understand there is in this house a spirit not at rest. Ghosts are merely manifestations of people who linger on after death. A tragic death involving a human sin often leads to encounters and malignant spirits can haunt a site of human vice.' He paused for a moment. 'I understand that may be the case with our dealings here. I shall attempt to confront the spirit and, using the power of our Lord, send it on to the next level. I shall then fill the space created by the presence of Christ.'

For a second he glanced away from the two men and his attention was taken by something high up under the gables, beyond the ivy. He could not say what it was that he saw but he felt it deep within him – a malevolence of a vile nature directed at himself. For the first time in his life Rev. Birtwistle knew fear.

'Gentlemen.' he continued gravely 'I have to tell you that I feel there is a strong force in this house. The devil himself is at work and we shall need all our faith and strength to overcome him. But conquer him we shall, with the power of prayer.'

He led the way to the door, opened it and fell to his knees. He asked God to be with him as he worked and to give blessing to his actions in His name. He asked that the powers of evil be put to flight and the angel of peace enter

144

the house. As he rose, once more his knees protested but standing in the wide entrance hall he felt more than just painful joints. There seemed to be an invisible, restrictive band all around him, seeking to render him helpless. Involuntarily, he tried to loosen his collar but the weight he had gained recently rendered his clothing unable to offer relief. The collar bit into his neck and his shirt was tight on his chest.

Rev. Birtwistle put his bag down on the flagstones and took out a wide necked phial of water. He felt faint but forced himself to continue. 'We ask O Lord that whatever is touched by this water may be purified from all that is evil or harmful.' He added four pinches of salt to the phial and prayed that when God's Holy Name was invoked, the devil himself would be repelled. The preparation of the holy water was complete.

Rev. Birtwistle took out from the bag an ornate crucifix on a chain and put it around his neck. He handed a large, white church candle to Captain Pollard and with the phial of holy water in one hand and the Bible in the other, he faced his comrades.

Taking a deep breath he said 'Gentlemen, let us commence.'

CHAPTER SEVENTEEN
The Exorcism

T HE clock in the hall struck nine as the three men ascended the stairs at Beesthorpe Hall. Captain Pollard felt great apprehension, simply because he didn't know what was going to happen, but if this was what was needed to restore domestic harmony, he would go along with it. He conceded that Wilhelmina must have witnessed something but he had taken tenancy of this house five years ago and he and his wife were totally unaware of a presence of any kind.

Cecil Smith-Woolley felt excited to be involved in a religious ceremony of such magnitude and relished the anticipation of the experience. His faith was absolute but he had only explored the dark side in discussion and he felt he was ready to be tested. He had total confidence in Rev. Birtwistle. They had known each other since setting up a local men's Christian Society and it was a good friendship, each admiring in the other qualities they did not possess themselves.

Rev. Birtwistle felt heavier of heart with every step. Why did this house and this spirit evoke in him such dread? How would this demon manifest itself? If only he didn't feel so ill. He wished he hadn't eaten so much at supper last evening. Mental and physical superiority were key issues in this encounter – the battle against evil. He did not feel up to the task, yet there was no choice as, inevitably, each step took him nearer the confrontation. He had cast out demons so many times before. Why lose his nerve now? Why this house?

On reaching the first landing, Captain Pollard indicated the second stairway leading up to the top of the house. A noise from behind startled them and they all froze. Captain Pollard remembered Richard and called out gruffly 'Is that you, Richard?' A mop of fiery red hair appeared on the stairs below. They all felt a little foolish and moved on.

The second staircase was narrow and steep and each step creaked in a menacing protest as they neared the upper landing. Rev. Birtwistle began to perspire and despite his mounting inexplicable fear, his pallor rose to a startling degree. His breath came in painful rasps and at the top step he held up his hand and said breathlessly 'A moment. A moment to recover my breath, if you please.'

The group stood close together. When the Reverend had recovered sufficiently they walked slowly down the corridor to the end door and stood observing it silently. The tension was palpable. Richard lurked behind, unwilling to join them, having decided it was only necessary to be within earshot.

The door looked innocent enough but what would be unleashed from within? The suspense grew and no-one spoke a word. Mr. Smith-Woolley produced the key, squared his shoulders and solemnly inserted it into the lock. He looked at the others, swallowed and started to turn the key. Nothing happened. It would not move.

'Locked for fifty years.' he said quietly 'Bound to be stiff.' Trying again, he pressed much harder and adjusted his body to put all his weight behind it. The loud clunk as the lock suddenly gave made them jump and a mixture of relief and anxiety flooded through the three of them.

'So. We have the door.' he exhaled slowly. 'Now we shall see.' The heavy door knob turned easily enough but the creak as Mr. Smith-Woolley pushed it as wide as it would go seemed to fill the whole house. A damp, fusty odour poured out but the three men, still standing on the threshold, peered inside for quite a few moments before their vision adjusted to the gloom. The small window on the far side of the room, covered in thick green mould and tatters of moth eaten cloth, allowed little daylight to penetrate. Layer upon layer of heavy cobwebs were festooned from sill to ceiling. Chunks of lime plaster had come away, exposing areas of reeds through which the rain had penetrated and stains had run down the walls, leaving big damp patches on the floor. At the side of the room stood the rusting frame of an iron bedstead. The mattress had been eaten through by mice and provided them with a handsome home. As the men stared and took in the details, a shape which they had perceived to be a piece of plaster suddenly moved. The tail of a large rat disappeared through a gaping hole. A foul odour enveloped them and its pungency stung their nostrils. Hesitantly, Mr. Smith-Woolley stepped inside and, fighting his way through the cobwebs, took the few paces over to the window.

'Well and truly jammed, I'm afraid.' he said pushing hard at it. His voice sounded hollow as it reverberated off the walls and into the empty space. 'What is this deplorable smell?' He took out a handkerchief and pressed it to his nose.

'Something that is rotting.' said the Captain grimly. 'Putrid flesh if my memory serves me correctly.' The silence of the room was overwhelming and no one spoke further. Their eyes took in all the details. Minutes ticked by and no one felt inclined to move. Mr. Smith-Woolley kicked a few pieces of plaster out of the way. Perhaps the room was not ready to give up its secrets, the Reverend thought to himself. Maybe if it was cleaned up and aired – Suddenly, with urgency the Captain called out 'Look to your feet, man!'

A dark, irregular shaped stain had begun to form around Mr. Smith-Woolley's feet as he stood in the middle of the room. He looked down in horror and then lifted his stricken face for guidance from Rev. Birtwistle. Paralysis temporarily overcame the Reverend and it was only through the utmost willpower that he managed to summon his strength and advance slowly into the room to stand by his friend's side. They both knew that the presence was here and they would be called upon to prove their faith.

'Enter with the candle.' Rev. Birtwistle's voice was shaky as he instructed Captain Pollard. Silently he prayed for strength. He must find it from somewhere to fight – to dominate this force which threatened to overpower his faith and himself. Physical and mental weakness now was unthinkable. Captain Pollard's spine tingled with fear as he tried to do as he was bidden. Gingerly, his hand shaking and sending the lighted candle flickering, he advanced with his head bent into the low-ceilinged room and the arena of the unknown. At last, finding a reserve of energy, Rev. Birtwistle employed his full oratorical vocal range and robustly embarked on the Lord's Prayer. Mr. Smith-Woolley joined in but found his mouth was dry and his words unconvincing. As they reached 'Deliver Us From Evil', the temperature dropped drastically and a tangible atmosphere of evil permeated the room.

'We are in the very presence of Satan himself.' thundered Rev. Birtwistle 'but he shall not prevail. I call upon the Holy God, The Holy Father and the Holy Spirit to stand by me.' The candle sputtered and whilst Captain Pollard struggled to contain his violent trembling, the jammed window flew open and a vicious blast of air extinguished it entirely. He felt himself pushed back against the wall and with horror realised that a sticky moisture was oozing from within it. The stain spread down the walls and congealed in a mass on the floor. With trembling hands Rev. Birtwistle took out the phial of holy water and uncorked it. He sprinkled it over the dark stain which instantly foamed and fizzled and turned into a bright red. The stains on the wall hissed and began to form an image. It swirled and entwined upon itself and finally revealed demonic eyes boring down and challenging Rev. Birtwistle as he stood before it with Bible and crucifix as his only protection. The eyes flashed with venomous hatred upon him, piercing in their intensity and lunging into his very soul. A violent pain spread right through his chest. He closed his eyes and waited for the pain to ease. As it did so, he looked across the room to see the image of a lovely girl, her hair a mass of golden curls. She smiled to him and opened her arms, beckoning him to her.

Making the sign of the cross, he ordered 'Be gone from this place every evil haunting and phantasm. Be banished and depart for ever every unclean spirit.' His voice sounded powerful and authoritative but that was entirely due to his years of experience. The two other men took comfort from this show of strength as they stood in the evil room and prayed vigilantly. In truth it took every ounce of the poor Reverend's courage and energy to even remain in the room. He felt an enormous force working against him.

The foaming stains hissed with rage and violence. A scream echoed deep from within the walls. As he faced the wall, the pretty girl appeared again. This time she was naked and splashed with blood. Her eyes were wild with fear and her mouth was open wide, emitting a piercing scream. The Reverend knew she was a manifestation sent to test him. He banished her from his sight and felt a heavy hand fall on his shoulder. The two men were on the other side of the room. The Reverend knew that on his shoulder was the hand of evil.

'Show yourself, servant of the Prince of Evil. You are locked into the place of your wicked deed and cannot reach the appointed higher level. Betake yourself to the appointed place, there to remain forever. Be gone in the name of Christ!' The Reverend battled on with the rite of exorcism. For hours he continued to wage his war amongst the chaos of the manifestations. With difficulty he read a passage from the Gospel of St. Luke as the edges of the pages of his Bible riffled under his hands. It was paramount that he should not give in. Chilled through yet perspiring, he shook visibly with the effort of will required to continue. Many times Mr. Smith-Woolley looked across at his friend, fearful that he would collapse at any moment. His voice would turn to a whisper and the words would not form but then from somewhere the strength would flood back and he would proceed to the next part of the ritual.

'May Almighty God deliver you from the powers of darkness and lead you into the light and obedience of Christ. Be gone, Satan, and cease to trouble this servant of God.'

Abruptly, just as the holy water was all but used up, a sudden silence befell the room. A stillness prevailed, only broken by the laboured breathing of the three men. The foul odour had gone, leaving only the smell of damp and mice. The stains diminished and quiet returned. Rev. Birtwistle remained in the centre of the room, the Bible clasped in his rigid white hands, unable to move. The stillness seemed just as menacing as the chaos. Each man felt their heart pounding and their breathing erratic. Eventually, Mr. Smith-Woolley recovered enough to ask quietly 'Is it over? Has it gone?'

He was the first to make a move and put his hand gently on the Reverend's arm. The human contact brought Rev. Birtwistle back to the moment and weakly he continued with a blessing of the room. Finally, he whispered 'The demon has gone to the appointed place. Go and find peace.'

CHAPTER EIGHTEEN
Retribution

ALMOST five hours had gone by when Richard came into the kitchen and announced to Cook and Wilhelmina that it must be over because they were coming down the stairs.

'Did you see anything. What happened?' asked Wilhelmina. She and Cook had worked half heartedly at their tasks, straining their ears for anything which might tell them what was going on. Once, she had even stood on the first landing but her courage had been short lived and she had quickly retreated to the safety of the kitchen.

'I didn't actually see anything myself.' Richard admitted. I kept well back but I heard things.'

'What things?'

Before he could speak Mrs. Pollard came through the door. 'Luncheon in half an hour, Cook. Wilhelmina, present yourself in the library in ten minutes.'

Cook looked down at the baked up crust of the beef pie and the sad boiled potatoes. 'Get me the butter, Winnie. We'll mash them.'

Down in the library, Rev. Birtwistle slumped into the armchair. He wouldn't even have made it down the stairs without the support of the others. He felt as though his life's blood had been drained out of him. This house meant nothing to him but he felt that it had been waiting a long time for his arrival and he had an inexplicable feeling of pre-destiny.

'I think, gentlemen' said Captain Pollard shakily, 'a cognac is called for.' He couldn't help spilling a few drops as he poured three large drinks. What a marathon of a ritual, he thought to himself. He'd had no idea that such

152

things could happen. He'd have to pay someone from the village to come and clear that room out. Someone who didn't know about it. He didn't like to think that he had lived in this house with that room above them all this time. He had no intention of telling his wife much about today.

'I must say alcohol is not something of which I generally partake.' said Mr. Smith-Woolley 'but perhaps on this occasion.' He took a gulp and appreciated the resulting inner glow.

'Purely medicinal, of course, Reverend.' murmured Captain Pollard as he offered the glass to Rev. Birtwistle who accepted it gratefully. 'Well, my word, what a turn of events. Quite a morning! Yes indeed.'

Rev. Birtwistle remained silent, his face devoid of expression, his energy depleted, but Mr. Smith-Woolley, restored by the alcohol, became a little more like his usual garrulous self. He endeavoured to embark on a theological discussion but had little support as Captain Pollard remained in a shaken bewilderment by the whole thing and the Reverend was still not up to conversing.

'You see' he reasoned, 'goodness is eternal. It integrates and edifies whereas evil disintegrates and destroys. Therefore, there can be no everlasting reality for evil. Goodness must be the dominant force.' He delivered this theory hastily and then sat in quiet contemplation, looking out of the window.

'Now, I think the kindest thing at this stage' ventured Captain Pollard, 'would be for us to summon Wilhelmina and inform her that the phenomenon has been addressed.'

This was agreed and soon the stocky laundry maid was standing before them to be given a bland version of the morning's events.

'So you see, there is nothing to fear. Everything has been dealt with by the Rev. Birtwistle here. Is that not so, Rev. Birtwistle?'

'What? Oh yes. Nothing to fear. The manifestation of a ghost is merely a cry for help. A haunting is simply a lost soul in need of direction.' He managed to smile encouragingly at Wilhelmina. 'With God's will, all will be well, my dear.'

The luncheon that Rev. Birtwistle had so anticipated was served in the large dining room where Mrs. Pollard joined them. The sombre Reverend sat at the huge table laden with food, his melancholy and preoccupied state prohibiting easy conversation. Mrs. Pollard mostly addressed herself to Mr. Smith-Woolley who ordinarily would have had no hesitation in giving his opinions on ghosts or any other subject but now, in the light of the recent shocking events, he found himself less able to pontificate in his usual flamboyant style.

Although the brandy had helped, a feeling of nausea still overwhelmed Rev. Birtwistle. He pushed the food around on his plate with a total disinterest. The beef pie had not been completely sacrificed by Cook and, under any other circumstance, would have elicited remarks of appreciation. But the morning had taken a great toll of him and food was the last thing on his mind now. He still felt constricted and uncomfortable and ran his fingers around his collar, looking forward to the moment he could depart this hateful house. Never in his life had he felt so ill at ease and this in itself was most unusual. Why was today so different? He had been blessed with a convivial, accepting nature which helped to overcome all obstacles of life, even those of such magnitude as today.

He longed to be in his own armchair back at Vicars Court, being fussed over by his housekeeper. He found his thoughts wandering to his childhood in Southwell, in the very same house in which he lived today. His parents unfailing love and pride in him had sustained him all his life. Through his father's faith he had found his own and his mother had taught him that service to others was the true meaning of love. In his head he could hear the sound of his parents voices as he gazed wistfully out of the windows of the dining room on to the green countryside. The persistent discomfort in his chest brought him out of his reverie and back to the troubled house. Secretly, he was not convinced that the exorcism had worked. It was quite possible that the spirit had quietened only temporarily and that events would recur at a later date. He made a decision there and then that if that proved to be the case he would not return to Beesthorpe Hall. The Bishop would have to find someone else to send in his place. He would never return.

Out in the orchard, Wilhelmina sat on a log, idly twiddling a bluebell between her thumb and fingers. She gazed thoughtfully back up to the house. It wasn't that she was frightened, but more that she didn't want to be where a spirit could be so unhappy as to make all those bad things happen. She would never forget that scream as long as she lived and the memory of the blood running all over the room made her shiver in the beautiful May sunshine.

'Hello, Winnie' Richard had come up behind her and sat down on the log.

'Whatever happened, it must have been really bad up there.' she said, indicating the top of the house. Richard absently plucked a couple of bluebells and examined them closely.

'Passions ran deep and the spirit just stayed I suppose. Now the Reverend has sent it on its way, it'll be alright – you'll see.'

Wilhelmina was not convinced, however encouraging other people's words. Suddenly she caught her breath and stared hard. The mangled bluebell dropped into her lap.

'Did you see it?' she asked urgently, her eyes transfixed on the attic windows of the house.

'What?'

'I don't know but for all the world it looked like – well, eyes. Flashing, angry eyes.' She turned to Richard, embarrassed to be sounding so dramatic. 'I know it sounds silly.'

There was absolutely nothing to see but Richard did not belittle Wilhelmina. He had been shaken by Jed's story and had thought a great deal about it. He had had little difficulty in picturing the horror and misery of fifty years ago but would never tell Winnie. Now as he scrutinised the house he was at a loss.

'Perhaps it was the sun flashing on the windows.' he offered. The early afternoon sun had come round to play on the back of the house, bathing it in warm shining light, but Wilhelmina remained sceptical.

'No.' she breathed. 'It was a warning. I know it.'

They sat in silence for a while, Wilhelmina going through in her mind's eye what she thought she had just seen and Richard, pondering the implications of the spirit still being there.

'I'm going.' she finally announced. 'To Newark. If I hurry I'll catch the carrier's cart.' She looked at Richard whose face showed unhappy resignation. 'I'll get work easily enough and I can find a place to stay for the night. I can't stay one more night here, Richard.'

'I'll miss you, Winnie.' he said, realising for the first time how much he enjoyed the company of this plain, dependable girl. Hesitantly, he reached out and gently squeezed her hand.

Wilhelmina smiled. 'Ask for me at the Royal Oak. I'll leave word there.' The decision made, she suddenly felt lighter and jumped up. Her dark, unruly hair became unpinned and tumbled down on one side and she reached up and half-heartedly tucked it back in. She hesitated as she held Richard's gaze and then said quickly 'I've made my mind up.' Running back through the orchard she

156

turned, waved and smiled at Richard and called out 'Don't forget – the Royal Oak' before disappearing to collect her things and hurry down the road to Caunton.

Richard remained sitting on the log. Something was nagging at the back of his mind. Perhaps he ought to go and see Jed again. As he pushed deeper into the spinney the bluebells became a carpet and the warmth of the day brought the heady scents of the flowers and the lush foliage together in a potent mix.

As Richard came to the hovel in the clearing there was no sign of Jed and no answer to his call.

'Jed! You, there?' he pushed on the door and stepped inside. The smelly old room that Jed had occupied for over fifty years had a different odour today. Waiting for his eyes to adjust to the gloom, Richard called gently and then made out a small movement under the rabbit-skin cover. He crossed over to the old man. Jed's breathing was laboured and his eyes were closed but gradually he became aware of a presence and opened them. He recognised his young friend.

'Can I fetch anything for you, Jed? Some of Cook's broth, perhaps?'

'No.' Jed shook his head wearily. 'Too late for broth.'

In a gesture of concern, Richard pulled up the fur blanket to cover him.

'I want you to have it – the rabbit-skin. I know you always liked it.'

Richard looked into the eyes of the dying old man and nodded. 'I should be honoured to have it, Jed. It's beautiful.' Jed nodded acknowledgement.

'I'm sorry I didn't do the job properly.' he breathed. 'The stake an' all. Just didn't seem right. Didn't mean no harm. Never thought McCready's ghost would walk. Tell Winnie I'm sorry.'

'It wasn't your fault, Jed.' Richard patted the old man's cold hand, trying to reassure him. 'There's a question I have to ask though. It's been at the back of my mind for a while now. Jed, what happened to the baby?'

'Baby? What baby?'

'Kitty's baby. You remember. You told me it was born in the workhouse. Did it die?'

A distant look came into the weak old eyes as he forced his mind to recall fifty years ago. His words were punctuated with gasps for breath and his voice little more than a whisper as he struggled to relate the final part of the story.

'Well now, that was a funny thing.' Making an effort, he focused on Richard.

'God must have really wanted that child to live. They left it to die but it didn't. The doctor came back later that day and when he saw it was still alive he took it away to be baptized.'

Richard felt guilty questioning such a sick man but pressed on with one more.

'What happened to the baby then?'

'Adopted. The vicar who baptized him. He and his wife had no children of their own. Brought up in Vicars Court. Southwell. Did well by him they did.'

'Him? A boy, then?'

Jed nodded, exhausted. His eyes closed but Richard shook his shoulder gently. 'What was the name, Jed? The people who adopted the baby?'

'Funny name. Can't remember. Oh yes. Birtwistle it was. I think it was Birtwistle.'

The seemingly interminable luncheon finished at last. Rev. Birtwistle's skin felt clammy with the exertion of remaining at the table. Mercifully, the afternoon sun did not find its way into the vast dining room but nevertheless he found it necessary to repeatedly mop his brow and wish for a cooler day.

Throughout the awkward meal, Mr. Smith-Woolley had begun to plan in his mind the speech he would deliver to the Mens Christian Society. His encounter with the spirit and his alliance with Rev. Birtwistle to propel it on to the next level, had both shocked and excited him greatly. He felt he had earned his spurs and who knew how many times in the future he may be called upon to provide a wall of faith in the face of an evil spirit?

'I bid you good-day, gentlemen.' he boomed in the hallway. Then, turning to Rev. Birtwistle he shook his hand warmly and said seriously, 'I have not overlooked the rigorous nature of your day's work and I can see the effort it has cost you. God speed until we meet again, my friend.' Turning to Captain Pollard he assumed the role of the land agent 'At last the locked room has been opened up and the spirit dispatched. Whatever happened there must have been vile indeed. Should you need me again just send word but I feel your household will now be more at ease.' He climbed aboard the trap waiting by the front door and with a final wave set off through the gates and down the drive at a cracking pace.

The Bishop's coach emerged from the stable courtyard. The spirited bays, refreshed, stamped their hooves impatiently on the stone slabs and the harness jingled as they tossed their heads, anxious to start their homeward journey.

'I cannot thank you enough, Sir, for the work you have done here today.' said Captain Pollard. 'This house will now be a safer place and our lives the easier for it.'

Rev. Birtwistle smiled feebly at his host. 'May God grant that I have completed His task.' As he picked up his bag and approached the carriage the horses reared and had to be steadied by the coachman, but he managed to negotiate the carriage step and sink gratefully, at long last, into the Bishop's upholstered seat. Captain Pollard closed the carriage door.

As the coachman struggled to maintain discipline over the excitable horses, he allowed them very slowly to ease around the circular drive. Why did Rev. Birtwistle choose that moment to lean forward and peer up at the house? The very house he did not wish to see ever again? Why did he not just close his eyes in the safety of the Bishop's carriage and allow himself to put the day's difficulties behind him? Something compelled him. An unknown force took command of his will and imposed upon him the glimpse of evil.

From high up in the house, eyes full of hatred and vile wickedness locked into his heart. Pain stabbed through him as instantly as the revelation before him. Like a lamb to the slaughter he had been led to this loathsome place. There was no other victim but himself, lured by the vanity of his faith. Why? Why should this house have such meaning and hold such fear for him.? God had stood by him all his life, leading him in the direction of the light but now it seemed that He was abandoning him to flounder, lost for eternity, on the dark side.

The Reverend's faith deserted him as the band of pain tightened and the disembodied eyes spewed forth their power, their supremacy, their domination.

'I am the Resurrection and the Life saith the Lord. Whosoever.....' the words died on his lips as the vomit inside him began to rise. He gasped with the pain and clutched his chest.

The horses by now had become more and more agitated. The weather-beaten face of the elderly coachman was alarmed as he used all his skills to try to calm them, but to no avail. They thrust their forelegs high into the air, whinnying and snorting as their flanks trembled, and then careered down the drive, the coach

160

lurching violently and threatening to overturn at any moment. The poor coachman, struggling to gain control over the manic beasts, used all his strength to haul on the reins. He was powerless to exert any influence over them as they hurtled along, heads high and ears laid back.

Suddenly, he felt the tension of the reins taken from him and as he looked down at his own calloused hands he saw that the reins were now in the strong, capable hands of the young coachman at his side. Soothing words came from somewhere, reassuring the agitated animals. They picked up the sounds and started to settle and slow down, their ears twitching and straining for the voice they could hear.

Along the road a pretty young girl walked, calmly oblivious to the drama. Her golden curls shone in the bright sunshine and bounced as she jauntily strode on. As the coach drew alongside she raised her lovely blue eyes and smiled a glowing smile at the young coachman with the boyish face and the floppy hair.

Slumped back in the seat Rev. Birtwistle felt a blanket of peace enfold him. The pain had gone and his face no longer reflected the fear he had felt. His God was with him and once more his faith was his guide, for on the journey he was about to make he would not be alone. Through half closed eyes he saw the pretty young girl and knew that she had come for him. Her identity he did not know. How could he? He had never seen the angelic face of his real mother. His adoptive parents had told him how much she had loved him and he had always treasured the old hazlenut with the faded red ribbon, but he was sure of one thing – God knew her and he had put his trust in God.

As if in slow motion, he pictured himself as a child, holding and caressing the shiny hazelnut, fingering the red ribbon and smiling to himself that his mother had loved him. That he had this day returned to the house and the very room of his conception was unknown to him. The reason for the venom personally directed at himself he could never have understood. His bastard birth, the result of one blissful encounter between two young people, was a source of immense anguish for the lost soul of John McCready. He had lured him here to put him under such emotional pressure as to cause his demise. The retribution so cruelly exacted on the father had been emulated for the son. At last, John McCready had had his ultimate revenge.

Cuthbert Birtwistle breathed his last, ignorant to the end that he was a child of the workhouse. His humble birth under tragic circumstances had been kept from him. That God had seen fit to equip that pathetic baby, born on a cold winter's night in the workhouse, with a tenacity for life, a compassion for others and the ability to do His work, was to prove the prophecy wrong.

Much good indeed had come about for this child of the workhouse. As a baby he brought joy to his adoptive parents, as he grew he brought them pride in his educational achievements and as a member of the church he brought solace and comfort to many. Against all odds, he had lived a good and happy life. The bleak prediction of 'only bad will come of the child of the workhouse', foretold out of ignorance and superstition, had been ill-founded.

The horses were now under control and the mystified old coachman, once more alone, urged them gently on. The blue sky of the pleasant afternoon changed abruptly as the horses trotted past the Caunton crossroads. From nowhere a heavy cloud obscured the sun and a sudden wind whipped the leaves of the ancient wych elm. Oblivious, the coachman was unaware that for his journey back to Vicars Court in Southwell that day, he was carrying the lifeless body of the much respected Reverend.

162

Captain and Mrs. Pollard sat in the drawing room at Beesthorpe Hall in the fading light. Mrs. Pollard put down her embroidery and addressed her husband.

'I just hope that word will not go out all over the county about this. And who would have thought that Wilhelmina, after all we have done, would still leave.'

'Do not distress yourself, my dear. I do assure you, all is now well. We shall find another laundry maid in no time.' He cleared his throat self consciously and continued. 'However, I have made a decision. Partly brought about by this event, I must concede – but one of which I think you may approve.' Mrs. Pollard sat perfectly still and waited. 'I think, my dear, we should both be happier if we were to return to Bristol. I feel disinclined to renew the tenancy here beyond September. May I take it that this would be acceptable to you?'

Mrs. Pollard's thin lips formed an icy smile and with a satisfied sigh she said 'Yes, Edward. That would be most acceptable.'

Captain Pollard allowed himself a moment to revel in his wife's approval before he continued. 'By the way, Richard informs me that the old gamekeeper died this afternoon. We'll bury him tomorrow and then clear away that old place of his.'

'Not before time.' was her only reply.

As night fell, a suffocating stillness descended on Beesthorpe Hall. Captain Pollard remarked upon it to his wife. Jed's body lay under his rabbit-skin shroud and the owls began their nightly calls. The bats flew out from under the eaves and high up at the top of the house on the attic bedroom floor, an irregular shaped stain slowly began to recede.